Praise fo

'Ahalya, Draupadi, Kunti, Tara, Mandodari – each of the Pancha Kanyas is fascinating. Ahalya's story has been told and retold several times, sometimes with varying accounts across texts. What was her relationship with Gautam and Indra? What was her crime? How was she redeemed? Why is she among the Pancha Kanyas? There have been modern retellings and interpretations too. Koral Dasgupta's wonderful retelling adds to this corpus, with a lyrical and poetic quality. The image that will remain with you is of the Mist ... Enthralling'

Bibek Debroy

'"Go, woman, find your world yourself. The joy you seek deserves to be discovered." Armed with this advice, Ahalya sets off on her life's journey. The magical and thought-provoking adventure that follows will intrigue and mesmerize readers'

Chitra Banerjee Divakaruni

'Koral Dasgupta's evocation of Ahalya, the first of the Pancha Kanyas, the five virtuous women from Indian myth, is an enigmatic tale about purity, chastity, seduction and redemption, told from the perspective of the eternal feminine'

Namita Gokhale

'Amazing premise and approach. This is one unique take on an age-old tale. Brilliant and intriguing'

Anand Neelakantan

'Impressed. I literally never imagined the interior world of a character from mythology in this way, let alone contemplating this way of reflecting on the soul, embodiment, desire and a woman's experience of the Brahma- and Indra-dominated worlds! Really powerful'

Prof Brian A. Hatcher

'In this original and spirited interpretation of the tale of Ahalya, Koral Dasgupta gives voice, character and agency to an enigmatic and fascinating female figure from ancient Hindu lore, while exploring and seeking to resolve the proverbial and vexing tension between asceticism and sensuality'

Prof Philip Lutgendorf

'Engaging and cinematic narrative'

Srijit Mukherjee

'A stream of consciousness; a spiritual telling. It rescued and redeemed the purity ruse. Koral is a visual writer'

Nabila Jamshed

'A stunning read. Fluent and engaging. What a fine writer!'

Fiona Sampson

'Panchakanya and other women, reinterpreted, is a most pertinent call. *Ahalya* is beautifully written and the little details and imagined conversations bring the character alive. I also enjoyed the almost surrealistic movement between mythical time and ours. It's a reminder that we in India live by a philosophy of transitions, an in-between-ness. Ahalya is amongst us'

Prof Malashri Lal

'Powerful ... The novelty of the novel lies in the fact that no other writer has talked about Ahalya vis-à-vis her womanhood'

Outlook

'In a most intriguing retelling, Dasgupta's narrative turns the seduction story on its head, making Ahalya the seducer instead of the seduced'

Scroll.in

'An ecocritical reading of *Ahalya* reveals the exploration of an ancient connection with nature that's sacred, intimate, and as we are in the midst of an environmental emergency, vital to reconcile with today'

Firstpost

'[T]he brilliance of Dasgupta's retelling is not just within the confines of that transformation itself, but rather, the importance of being seen, validated and loved as you are'

Southern Humanities Review

'Koral Dasgupta creates true wonder with her new book *Ahalya*'

Tempest

'A stunning piece of literature'

Dipannita Sharma

Praise for *Kunti*

'Koral Dasgupta writes about Kunti, one of the Pancha Kanyas, with verve, emotion and passion. Her highly readable account of this fascinating character, who played a key role in the Mahabharata, is a must for those wishing to know about our past and the dialectics of gender within it'

Pavan K. Varma

'Koral Dasgupta makes the ancient myths speak in new and unexpected voices; voices that have been lost and sunken in the dominant narrative consciousness, and yet, the voices of characters who made the flesh, blood and the values of the epics possible'

Saikat Majumdar

'Bringing heroines of yore, like Ahalya and Kunti, to contemporary times, Koral Dasgupta writes with a rare verve and energy. Never dull or pedantic, she makes the woman within the legend come alive. A rare talent'

Makarand R. Paranjape

Praise for *Draupadi*

'*Draupadi* lives up to the expectations set by *Ahalya* and *Kunti* ... Koral [Dasgupta] dares to boldly push the narrative in ways you cannot imagine. A must-read'

Kiran Manral

'This is a striking rewriting of Draupadi's story. Koral Dasgupta has given us a Draupadi who is fearless, politically astute and unwilling to be anyone's victim. This Draupadi leans into her power and changes the course of history in Dasgupta's beautifully crafted world'

Prof Tracy Pintchman

'In poetic prose Koral Dasgupta weaves surprising threads into the ever-evolving tapestry of the Mahabharata, enriching it with this empowering, lyrical telling of Draupadi's life'

Prof Hillary P. Rodrigues

'Koral Dasgupta has given us a unique take on a well-known story from the Mahabharata. It is fascinating to hear this tale from a female perspective, to hear [Draupadi's] thoughts and struggles about being offered in marriage to all five brothers, as well as her eventual realization of the purpose behind the marriage. This work clearly shows Draupadi to be an intelligent and rational player in the divine plan. In our attempts to make the academic world more diverse and accessible to all, a reading of Draupadi alongside the Mahabharata would be an excellent way to open new dialogues in the classroom and beyond'

Prof Arnold Smit

'This lyrical and insightful reimagining of Draupadī's narrative is a worthy entry in the long tradition of telling the tales of India's (and the world's) great epics'

Prof Brian Collins

'A lively series of beloved stories from ancient India that speak to modern readers'

Prof Paul B. Courtright

Praise for *Mandodari*

'Imaginative, intense and insightful ... Narrated in Koral's signature style, the exchanges of Mandodari and Sita (and their implications for Ravan and Ram) are absolutely fascinating'

Ashwin Sanghi

'[*Mandodari*] has several strengths, including, but not limited to, Dasgupta's envisioning of the inner world of the women of Lanka, the differences, sympathies and alliances within, as well as the titular character's moral turbulence'

Telegraph

'*Mandodari* with its lyrical prose and philosophical moorings ... conjures up visions of a mesmerizing world. The book shows how so much is made possible by a lone woman's resilience and unswerving commitment to do the right thing'

New Indian Express

Praise for *Tara*

'Embedded within the epic saga of the Ramayan, *Tara*'s nuanced narrative is bathed in grace and empathy. We enter the non-textual world of the vanaras to discover a deep worldview through the voice of an extraordinary protagonist'

Namita Gokhale

'A powerful depiction of Tara's world, encompassing Bali and Sugreev, with distinct ideologies influencing the rules of the Kishkindha kingdom'

Amish

'Exuberant and imaginative, this narrative about kinship, friendship and love explores questions about borders: between the animal and the human, the wild and the tame, the living and the dead, the revelatory and the remembered, heaven and earth, language and silence. With a cast of vividly etched characters and a feel for the mysteries that lie at the heart of intimacy, here is a fascinating tale by an inventive and thoughtful storyteller'

Arundhathi Subramaniam

DRAUPADI

KORAL DASGUPTA has published an eclectic range of books, from academic non-fiction to relationship dramas. Her books are discussed in the context of gender studies, art, myth and ecocritical literature. Other than India, Koral's books can be found in the libraries of Harvard University, Columbia University, the University of Pennsylvania, University of Chicago, University of Wales, Duke University, University of North Carolina, Texas A&M University, among others. The books in the Sati series have been nominated for various prestigious awards, with *Ahalya* most recently being recommended for the 2023 Sahitya Akademi Prize Honour List.

Koral is the founder of www.tellmeyourstory.biz and conducts writing programmes and critical thinking workshops for educational and corporate floors. She has been recognized on the Innovator25 Asia Pacific 2019 list prepared by the Holmes Report and featured in the Women of Wonder (WOW) series in *Outlook Business* magazine.

Her website is www.koraldasgupta.com.

Also in the Sati series

Ahalya

Kunti

Mandodari

Tara

DRAUPADI

KORAL DASGUPTA

THE SATI SERIES III

PAN

First published 2022 by Pan
an imprint of Pan Macmillan Publishing India Private Limited
707 Kailash Building
26 K. G. Marg, New Delhi 110001
www.panmacmillan.co.in

Pan Macmillan, The Smithson, 6 Briset Street Farringdon, London EC1M 5NR
Associated companies throughout the world
www.panmacmillan.com

ISBN 978-93-90742-54-7

This is a work of fiction. Names, characters, businesses, organizations, places, events, and incidents either are the product of the author's imagination or are used fictiously. Any resemblance to actual persons, living or dead, events, or locales is entirely coincidental.

13

Typeset in Guardi LT Std by R. Ajith Kumar, New Delhi
Printed and bound in India by Replika Press Pvt. Ltd.

MIX
Paper | Supporting responsible forestry
FSC™ C016779
FSC www.fsc.org

For my son, Neev Tanish

CONTENTS

SERIES INTRODUCTION

The Pancha Kanyas of Hindu mythology are Ahalya, Kunti, Draupadi, Mandodari and Tara, while the five Satis include Sita, Sati, Savitri, Damayanti and Arundhati. The distinction between these two different titles arose primarily because certain versions of the epics have taken the liberty to celebrate women as per the popular beliefs of their era and, of course, those of the translators. One school of thought defines 'Sati' as symbolizing the women's unconditional devotion to and dependence on their men. It casts the women as loyal followers, strongly supporting the vision of the men around them or helping them overcome social and emotional challenges. These women are depicted as self-sacrificing and selfless, yet invincible when drafting their own position of strength and authority.

Various senior scholars translate the Pancha Kanyas as 'five virgins'. Thus, based on textual evidence, the Kanyas and Satis are different women. However, in the earliest texts, there is no mention of the Pancha Satis; they only talk about the Pancha Kanyas who are deemed as the Maha Satis. Even in regional interpretations, especially in some eastern and southern states of the country, this division is blurred. This could be due to the difference in the spread of the Mahabharat of Vedavyasa versus the dissemination of Valmiki Ramayan. The former specifically mentions the Pancha Kanyas.

Many versions of the Ramayan discuss the Satis in terms of loyalty and physical chastity. Such women, including Sita, aren't restricted to only five. But they don't club them under the umbrella term, Pancha Sati. In my own studies, I came across some scholarly assumptions that the Satis were reborn as Kanyas, with research trying to draw parallels!

An ancient *shloka* establishes that reciting the names of the Pancha Kanya can dispel sins, which again confirms the 'Sati' status of these women. Sati, meaning pure, devoted and fair. Purity that cannot be destroyed by external influence, because criticism or judgment cannot deflect one from her chosen path of righteousness.

In the Sati series, I follow this conception of 'purity' while retelling the stories of the five illustrious women: Ahalya, Kunti, Draupadi, Mandodari and Tara. The purity that is brave enough to present itself the way it is – sans any cosmetic cover – and mirrors the mind unpretentiously as much as it exposes the politics of a society.

However, the Sati series is not meant to be biographical. The purpose of the series is to draw attention to a part of the journeys of these legendary women that have been grossly overlooked. Identities have been imposed based on incidents that the patriarchy considered criminal, shameful or irresponsible. When these known events adopt the narrative voice of a feminine titular character, the stories change. The world expands. The Sati series not only presents an inclusive overview of the protagonist's own life but also dives deep into the suppressed pain of those around them – be it a man or a woman.

In the first, fourth and fifth book of the series, *Ahalya, Mandodari* and *Tara,* the entire narrative had to be recreated. About Kunti and Draupadi, a lot is known already. My retellings spotlight the making of these characters, albeit from a non-traditional perspective, which ushers the readers into a new era of thinking and reimagining.

Ahalya introduced the woman as a lover. Ambitious, futuristic, royal and calculative; not afraid to express, nor hesitant to ignore the binding rules of the world. *Kunti* called for a relook at the patriarchal origins of 'Mata' and, in relation, the pervasive sociopolitical image of the sacrificing Indian mother. *Draupadi* was even more complicated than the previous books because it shed light on the societal reactions across generations towards crimes against women, particularly those who are successful. *Mandodari* sparked yet another powerful discourse on the critical choices faced by an accomplished woman between the calls of of her mind and heart, in light of a terrible sin committed by her extremely talented husband. *Tara,* the last book of the series, brings up the discourse of human–animal politics, highlighting the grandeur of certain traditions of the forest and the wisdom of animals that transcends boundaries. It also explores the sensitivity that prompts a woman to forgo the blinds borne by the diplomatic crown of a queen.

Ram's killing of Bali while hiding behind a bush is a disturbing episode from the Ramayan that I personally could never digest. Tara's narrative opens with an acknowledgement of Bali's death and then travels through the sequence of events – securing some emotional and logical derivatives.

PROLOGUE

'Krishna?'

'Yes, Krishnaa.'

'Why do you call me that?'

'Because it sounds like I am you. And it confuses others.'

'The other day I caught some temple gossip – the devotees were whispering that Draupadi was Sita in her earlier birth!'

'Were you?'

'Maybe. Who knows? Returned to the earth to be reborn from fire!'

'If that is true, Ram must also be around. He will come back to clear the pending debts. He is answerable to Sita. Birth after birth he'll follow

> *her, to seek forgiveness and follow her commands, which he couldn't as a husband.'*
>
> *'Can Ram ever bring justice to Sita?'*
>
> *'She is far bigger than him.'*
>
> *'If I am Sita, I wouldn't marry Ram if he comes looking for me.'*
>
> *'Don't. Let him be insignificant in your world, serving as a slave, always at your beck and call.'*

I don't remember since when I have known Krishna or who introduced me to him. He was just there. The eternal flute pulsated through the air, whether or not I paid attention. From the pond below the balcony, or the palace dairy, sometimes across the river or from further away down the plains, always carrying a timbre of jubilance. The tune teased from afar when I sat in the palace garden with my friends, our childhood banters interspersed with vigorous laughter. It was the dominant music during my *swayamvar* – though heard by only one other. The relentless melody flattened the steep challenges of the matrimonial world where each person had illustrious glory to flaunt and ignominious failures to hide. I searched for happiness in this overtly agitated sphere and drifted into the orbit of creation. Of relationships, of a kingdom, of a home.

And then, one day, the music of my heart changed its course. The melody of the flute was replaced by the call of the conch.

After my birth, astrologers had prophesied that Draupadi would be accused of bringing fierce destruction upon a clan of furious warriors. Only a few thoughtful historians would revisit the ruins to unmask the magnificent past destroyed in a monstrous massacre. The rest would be misinformed visitors and manipulative observers relaying twisted versions of my story. Poor things. I sympathize with these storytellers. Innumerable words would fill up their blank pages in a rigorous attempt to affix my identity. The queen of Indraprastha. Princess of Panchal. Daughter of Dhrupad. Arjun's beloved. Kunti's protégé. Bhishma's darling. Krishna's muse. An ultimatum for the Evil. A fantasy for everyone else. As much as the scripts glitter with impressive alliterations, the gaps between their words would ridicule the ink of inconclusiveness. I will excuse the future for its confusion, though. A woman who smelt of blue lotuses at birth and left behind the stench of burning corpses mid-way into her life – the contradiction could convolute the judgement of the generations to come. Writers will shut and reopen the case from time to time. I will still refuse to fit into their word counts.

> *'I thought you are fond of the intellectuals, Krishnaa?'*
>
> *'Krishna, you are hence charged with psychological espionage!'*
>
> *'I don't need to spy on you. Your thoughts are loud.'*
>
> *'Louder is your intrusion.'*

*

Only a few days were left for the great war of Kurukshetra to begin. I lay on the bed of our tent, half my attire on the body, the rest on the ground. The thick cloth ceiling turned transparent to screen the black, overcast sky devoid of stars. The morning hours had arrived, but the world was still enveloped in darkness. The breeze was sparse, the owls awake, the leaves of the trespassing branches motionless. Sleeping birds inside the quiet cavities of trees were woken up by obnoxious harbingers signalling the arrival of dawn. Porcupines stealthily climbed up the uneven trunk of a peepul tree, only to race back down upon spotting a deadly viper coiled up on the topmost branch, waiting lazily for a prey to walk into its snare. The bats were having a noisy reunion. I could see them all. Who knows whether all these life forms would exist after the war? Or would the formalities of the vibrant world witness an irreversible change?

Hissssssss!

I looked up to trace the terrifying sound. Frustrated by its inaction, the hungry viper had spat at the surrounding leaves, turning them black with its acidic venom. Nothing new. That's how power operates; the wrath of the mighty is often inflicted upon the harmless. Would the tree punish the antagonist for its transgression? Or would it continue to suffer because, if dethroned from its venerable position, the viper would cause greater damage to those living below?

The flames from the earthen lamps placed in the western side of the tent danced to their own rhythms. On a gloomy night devoid of winds, the shadows were shaking, rising and falling rapidly to some tantric mystery. The inherent spark of togetherness where stimulants are redundant. The light and the shadow. Like me and Arjun. I knew he would come, though every ritual in the living world tried to suggest otherwise. Howsoever complicated be the engagements for the pre-war strategizing with the army, Arjun wouldn't leave for Kurukshetra until I bade him farewell.

The hours were inching towards *shakra amavasya* when the moon would be in Indra's star of *Vishakh*. Every amavasya night had seen a surge in my vigour ever since the kingdom of Hastinapur had dishonoured itself through a courtroom menace wherein the evil attempted to disrobe a woman. Witnessed by a world of audience, the response to the incident was divided. Many spat at the king and his clan, blaming them for shameful tolerance of criminal campaigns. But the royalty of Hastinapur inspired its allies to consider using the historic disgrace as a potential weapon for stripping the confidence of the opponent. Many men from distant lands, seated in lavish quarters on either side of the sea, were citing the fabulous formula devised by the shrewd in the Maha Bharat.

Almost every weapon, though, comes with a counter. My dark skin glistened in fury, eyes blood red, open hair streamed down with unruly valour, footsteps raised wails from the cremation ground. The corrupt were yet to experience the blood and sacrifice with which the sins of the great Bharat would be cleansed in the same land.

I stood up to observe the darkness outside. A thousand *yakshi*s sighed at the masculine fragrance crossing their path, his eyes hooked on his destination. Arjun entered in hushed footsteps – playful and ever-flirting, be it bed or battlefield!

Ice-cold fingers pierced through my dense hair, stroking my back. His arm circled gently around my neck, my back pressing against his bare chest. The love was addictive, overwhelming. I hadn't removed my gaze from the grimness outside, but he seemed neither restless nor perturbed. The silence was titillating. There was no haste, though our time was not infinite. The endurance of a proud prince turned every passing moment into one of perennial loss if his wife didn't lavish complete devotion on him. But Arjun would never ask, let alone urge. He could disown with infuriating indifference, everything that was meant to be his. There would be no reluctance on his part if politics merited such benevolence.

Just like he had let go of me once, to honour a slip of tongue!

1

Dressed in a royal attire, bedecked with jewellery and a thick lace of jasmines entwined around my hair, I stepped inside the thick woods of the Dvaita forest soon after our wedding. Having narrowly escaped a murderous attack orchestrated by their Kaurav cousins at Hastinapur, the Pandav were camping here after spending a long period at the Kamyak forest. The kingdom of Indraprastha had not been founded yet. With the tip of my fingers, I tickled the bulging veins on the wrist of Arjun, the third Pandav and now my husband. A mischievous smile spread on his lips.

Mother Kunti stood at a distance watching

the setting sun, facing away from us. When the brothers called, she didn't turn around. Only saying, 'Whatever is brought must be shared between the five brothers equally.'

Shocked, the brothers looked at each other uncomfortably and dispersed. I stood there numb. Weren't they taking a silly misunderstanding too seriously?

Not much time was wasted in interpreting the mother's words as a command for me to marry all five brothers. The wedding garland hanging from my neck suddenly felt heavy, a sharp twinge radiated from the back of my neck. I split the thread holding together the flowers and let it drop to the forest floor. The elderly lady pretended to hear only the chirrup of the homecoming birds. She made no attempts to correct herself.

*

'How could you?'

I lashed out the moment we had some privacy. Trees of the Dvaita forest hurled dry leaves at me, reprimanding the resentment of a new bride. I pushed them away with a leg. Those days I was lost in love, yearning to be held in his majestic arms. But the finest archer of the land turned quite sluggish when it came to articulation. His silence, though, wasn't something I would settle for.

'How can I be split between the brothers? I am not a slice of mango to pleasure starved tongues.' I was angry, hurt and unsettled, looking for the rudest of words to torment my beloved.

Arjun caressed my shoulder as if I was a child whining over her lost toy. He stretched himself on the grass of the forest, tempting me with the spread of his toned body, looking skywards with a naughty glint in his eyes. My hands were itching to feel the warmth of his rising and falling chest. But they sat obediently on my lap, the bangles tinkling as I fidgeted now and then. Arjun smiled, forming a light dimple on his left chin.

'You are tough, Panchali,' he attempted a vague compliment.

Toughness, of all things! What else was I expecting from a warrior? He leaned towards me, eyes drunk with desire even as he remained aloof, unwilling to relinquish his stubborn restraint. 'The challenge at your swayamvar wasn't for one ordinary human to crack. It summoned the forces of five worlds,' he whispered in my ear.

There was a mysterious smile pasted on his lips; he was looking at the trees standing afar. I turned Arjun's face towards me and held it firmly between my palms. His cheeks, covered with a soft growth on the sides, writhed under my impolite touch. He looked like a child waiting to be loved. I was offended.

'What does that mean?' I demanded. He took my right hand in his and placed it on his bare chest. My dark fingers on his fair skin made for a ravishing contrast. There was something unusual about his touch – supporting yet unbending. I tried to pull away. The fingers refused to move as if they were no longer mine.

'Your swayamvar had a revolving fish hung from a pole. All contenders were to attempt piercing its eye with an arrow after studying only its reflection in the water below,' Arjun reminded.

'Such a terrific condition called for five occult forces. Dharamraj Yudhishthir followed the protocol of submitting to the princess first. Bhim, the son of Vayu, studied the temperament of the wind, which controlled the motion of the hanging object. Nakul charmed all with his looks and Sahadev shared his knowledge of physics. In this entire design, I was only the actor–executor tasked to hit the target.'

He looked at my shocked face with kindness. We both lay quietly on the grass. My eyes were focused on nothing, while my brain was muddled with a billion thoughts resisting the words I had just heard. I didn't want the argument to end. I wanted a fight.

Arjun kept seducing from a distance, arousing in my body the desires I didn't know existed. I still refused to budge.

'I will not love five men,' I was adamant.

'Then don't. Just love me.' He shocked again with a simple solution to the blasphemous problem. I wanted to get up and leave, annoyed by his riddles and his restraint, both. Forlorn eyes trapped me within obstinate boundaries, melting my resolve. I inched closer instead. His voice sent a ripple through my veins.

'We – the five brothers – are a network of nerves around the same skeleton. You will soon discover this and more.'

Leaves embossed with colourful designs on their blades came flying towards us. Arjun gathered a few and weaved them between my braid. 'It is complicated,' I heard him say. 'But convince yourself, Panchali. When you are with Yudhishthir or any of my brothers, you aren't away from Arjun.'

I didn't believe him; he could see it in my eyes.

'How?' I asked scornfully.

He touched my shoulder with his palm, strangely unroughened by fanatic archery. It smelled of lavender. He noticed I was distracted. 'It is an enormous *indrajal* known by none in the family or the country. The truth of yore, constructed carefully by the cult of Devraj Indra and never to be documented in history. You are in possession of the whole – what the rest of the world can only receive in parts.'

Before I could figure out whether this was yet another illusion created by the son of Indra, I was taken in by the lavender's lure and our mouths touched, bringing the evening's dialogue to a close.

*

That day and today – so much had changed! We matured in love but failed to protect our innocence. Yet, a few things remained unaltered. One was Arjun's focus on the present. He gave himself to it completely, as if nothing else existed. Inimitable commitment; one person at a time.

A world of aspirants would be kept in waiting – from kings knocking for help, Brahmins orphaned by destroyed *ashrams*, to audacious fathers with youthful daughters waiting to be married off. Even the wildlife from dense forests and below the sea came seeking mitigation to their problems. Outside our suite at Indraprastha, our children would raise the roof on their heads. Everything they needed would require the latch to our chamber to be unlocked. Their attendants cajoled them towards other unemployed toys with little success. They clonked on the closed door and ran away. Half-sitting on the bed with a hand covering his eyes, Arjun asked if the treasury could afford an extension to his armoury.

Soon after we shifted to Indraprastha, Mother Kunti had instructed, 'Hand over the keys of the treasury to her.'

Why, many wondered, but no one dared to ask.

The treasury was overflowing. Arjun's extended armoury would cause no dent. I still scowled. 'The armoury is already colossal.'

Removing the hand from over his eyes, he glared as if his darling wife's extravagance had been heartlessly challenged by some immoral monster. I tried not to laugh.

'There is a crowd calling out to you. Why aren't you responding?' I nudged.

'I can't hear them.' He sat up suddenly and pulled me into the bed, stroking my chin like a smitten lover. I blushed. He would attend to all later, I was sure, because none of the seekers ever came back to repeat their plea.

'Then what do you hear? Only the twang of the bow?' All morning he had spent burnishing his weapons with oil and sawdust till I barged in and pulled him out for lunch. He was resting his head on my lap now for a brief siesta, expecting my fingers to run through his dense hair. My fingers were far more friendly to him than I was.

'Have you ever heard an arrow cutting through the air? With the elegance of a flying eagle, louder than the parakeet?' he asked dreamily, caressing the back of my hand. 'It's rare, sharp and musical.'

Musical ... arrow. I rolled my eyes. His thumb moved over my lips. 'Your voice is like that, all-engulfing for the targeted audience.'

I withdrew abruptly, making his head fall on the bed from my lap. Arjun's compliments were always obnoxious. More enraging was his chuckle.

'What?' I charged at him.

'Nothing. The arrow has struck its target. My arrows always do.' He covered his eyes again, irritating me more.

'A messenger from Dwarka has been waiting

since morning. Met him?' I said casually as if this was about the taste of lunch.

'What?' he sprang up, 'Why—' and he stopped. A cold stare followed with him swearing my prank would receive a befitting retaliation. I laughed, pushing him off.

No outsider was allowed to enter our premises. Krishna was the only presence who never left. Arjun, the Pandav administrator, reported not to his eldest brother Yudhishthir, but to Krishna, his cousin from Dwarka!

*

Fearsome sounds of restless winds travelled from the grounds of Kurukshetra and headed towards my window, crossing many open meadows in between. They left course marks on my dehydrated skin, touching like the sigh of ancestors and pleading something indistinct. No birds flew in the barren sky, not a single reptile moved on the dusty lands. We were approaching the auspicious day when the final settlement was about to begin.

Arjun smelled divine. Ayurvedic elements were smeared all over his body, instilling calm and poise at every step. I let go and fell behind on his broad chest.

'Panchali!' he whispered.

The voice was not his alone. Five warriors were waiting to be energized by the Yagnaseni[1]. I turned and touched him. Hiding behind a confident smile was a throbbing, tense heart craving for the tender shelter of the feminine. We gazed into each other's eyes, sinking into the beauty of our togetherness and conscious of the unthinkable suffering both of us had brought upon each other. Yet, neither ever stopped loving the other. The love led us through many hostile rivers where crocodiles flocked to tear out flesh, junking stripped skeletons. We had finally reached a juncture where justice could be neither delayed, nor denied. The darkness would end soon. We would detach from the painful memories forever. Indifference heals better than forgiving.

---

[1] Another name of Draupadi, meaning, emerged from and refined by sacrificial fire.

We drifted towards a bed of grass devoid of any luxury our attendants used to once set up before our evenings of union. Now, we only had ourselves adorning each other. The hours passed in haste. For days after, we would be in separate camps. I would have no husband to love, only a warrior to be proud of.

Somewhere in the vicinity, Krishna's conch blew loud and long, each call mightier than the one before. The sharp bellows went up like a zestful child woken up to a life full of possibilities.

Conspirator! I murmured, hugging Arjun dearly before smearing his forehead with the *rakta chandan.*[2]

[2] Rakta chaṇdan means blood-red sandalwood, which is used especially to worship Kali. It is a symbol of annihilation of evil forces.

2

A great war doesn't take place on an opportune day because a troupe of gallant warriors are waiting for an assignment. It builds over time, involving dynasties with overlapping obstacles that lead to a deadlock. The royalty of Panchal had started preparing for the Kurukshetra much before my arrival in the world.

Panchali. The name had come to me not because I was the princess of Panchal but because I was obligated to its soil, Father Dhrupad had said. Bothered with something perpetually, he was steeped in frustration, as though to correct a horrific past that stung him like poison – its presence lethal but riddance tricky! His conflict with Dronacharya was known to all. He erupted at everyone who reminded him of his childhood friend, now an arch-rival. On many nights, I woke up startled to find Father seated on the floor with his back towards me, his head resting against my bed, close to my left hand, and eyes sealed to the ceiling. Beside me, Shikhandini would be fast asleep, having tamed wild elephants all through the day. Caught in such uncomfortable togetherness, I wasn't sure how I could help and he was too embarrassed to ask.

That year, the eastern part of Panchal was complaining of a possible drought if rains continued to be uncertain. While returning from a visit one day, I was weighing the available solutions to revive the abundance of the fertile land. The call of the mystic dissolved the discourse. Alluring, indulgent, loving. It mingled with the cool, moisture-laden air. Surprised, I climbed out of the palanquin. The drizzle fell like gentle blessings. By the time I entered the royal premises, heavy rains were washing down the palatial corridors. Had someone heard our prayers? The land would be green, paddy crop would soar and kitchens would be colourful again. I ventured out into the lawn, gleefully treading across the garden towards the violently shaking trees, God knows searching for what. At some corner of the palace, Shikhandini and Drishtadyumn were practising sword fighting; their hoots competed with the thrums of the downpour. My skin, always warmer than others', welcomed the cool streams trickling down. The monsoon fell like a doting patriarch, caressing my hair and gently cleansing muddy hands. The more I received the affection, the more I longed for it. I was searching for the open plains, where the raindrops would be unbarred from the tree trunks and their interlocking branches above. That's when an attendant came rushing, requesting me to return. My eyes went upwards. From behind the shaking branches and jubilant leaves, I could see my father standing on the balcony, looking very upset. Unwillingly, I followed the attendant. As I walked past him, dripping the water from my wet clothes onto the clean floor, he passed a look of stern disapproval. I chuckled.

At night, insomniac depression drove him to my chamber again. When he got up to leave around dawn, I caught his hand, surprising him.

'Father,' I said, 'The rains mesmerize me.'

He looked downwards at my response to a question he had never asked.

'I know,' he said sadly. 'But still, fathers try to stop their daughters. The forces are seeking you. You are willing to go with them. Fathers can't change things; they still try.'

'What do you want to change, Father?' I asked, amused.

He didn't smile; his face darkened. 'I wish I could change that I am a king and you are a princess. I wish I could correct the past. I wish my daughter was not plunged into the disorders of others' lives. Destiny has chosen you and, as much as I tried to resist it, you didn't.'

The next time I ran out of the palace to welcome the monsoon, I whispered, 'Who are you?'

'A messenger sent by your divine mate, wonderful,' a discreet whistle reverberated through the rustling leaves. The rain went from mild to vigorous; the shaking trees pretended to hear nothing.

'How is he, whom you call my divine mate?' I asked playfully.

'As cleansing as this downpour.'

A gust of wind blew past me. The mystic was chaining me into something enchanting.

Each time King Dhrupad would call me back, interrupting the conversations. But the more he cautioned me to stay away, the more I chased it. Surrounded by the wise men of the kingdom, with my birth charts spread before them, he'd pace up and down the corridor, mumbling things to himself.

*

'Krishnaa!'

The voice, like the music of the flute, echoed through the queen's chamber at Indraprastha.

'Done with politics for the day, conspirator?'

I asked in lieu of the friendship I had acquired as an incumbent of Panchal and firmed as a gift of my marriage to the Pandav. A bond that allowed me to say anything without hesitation. With him, I was neither a princess, nor a queen, a sister, daughter or wife. Not even a woman. With him I was me, or just no one. What inspired such confidence, I couldn't tell. Krishna was clueless about the formalities of a distinguished relationship.

He laughed every time I called him a conspirator. I loved to hear the echo of his laughter. It travelled from one chamber to the other, teasing the fire of glowing torches, making cryptic symbols with shadows on the walls, passing through the balconies and fading into the horizon.

> *'If I didn't conspire, Krishnaa, you would be stranded at the Panchal auditorium now, amid the stale flowers from your swayamvar. 'I made soulmates unite and you call it a conspiracy ...'*
>
> *'Really?'*

Krishna had initiated another mischievous fight. No one could win these debates with him; or perhaps everyone did. The dialogue was the trophy.

'You would have got me married to one of the cows in your herd as long as it was birthed by your feisty aunt. You brought me here for Mother Kunti. Arjun, you have reserved for yourself first.'

Caught blatantly, Krishna went back to his flute, playing it in spurts. Isn't this why I call him a conspirator? He turns to the instrument every time he wants to silence the world around. Everything shifts to the surreal, retaining no proof of the words exchanged. But the subconscious is awake, where everything hidden lies bare, where nothing that is said or heard can ever be forgotten. Within that fantasy world, knowledge is recycled into wisdom.

'Why do you keep going back to Panchal, Krishnaa? What lies incomplete there?'

'The misery of my father. I know every statistical detail about our kingdom. My father, however, I don't know well.'

The music pulled me along to travel during those nightly hours at Panchal, when Father would quietly come and sit near my bed, trying to say something but feeling abandoned by words.

I smelled smoke. Was anything burning? Intense, fluctuating flickers made a crackling noise. Dense, black fumes wriggled around. My beautiful retreat was clean and well maintained, with not a speck of dust in any corner. Outside the window, a woodpecker tirelessly drilled holes into an oak tree. The noise was consistent and exhausting. I had heard about the old oak in our garden, which had shed its leaves and whose roots had dried up. They brought it down the day I was born. The wood of the dead tree had been turned into a fine cabinet in my chamber. It had delicate designs crafted on its borders with a huge mirror rivetted in front. That cabinet was missing. Also missing from the walls were the hand-painted motifs of birds and blossoms and humans in yellow, orange and red that Shikhandini and I had made together. My wall had flowery grasslands balancing bounteous orchards with ripe fruits being desired by the chakor above and the peacocks below. Euphoric rivers ran from either end. Shikhandini's wall was full of handsome horses and gallant warriors, their faces masked by the clouds of earth raised by the runners. In the absence of those, the walls looked naked.

This looked like another era! I was trapped inside a strange bubble – a translucent enclosure. The clean outer world was a haze apart while I suffocated within the claustrophobic snare. Restlessly, I looked for an exit, pushing against the dividing wall with all my might, only to invite another rush of black winds upwards and inwards. I coughed and fanned them off, peeping through the wall again. King Dhrupad was sitting on the floor just like he used to. Attendants entered freely, unlike our times when Shikhandini didn't appreciate unsolicited company inside our private abode.

The music of the flute was mild, almost inaudible.

> *'Krishnaa, you have entered the Creator's womb!'*
>
> *'Creator's womb? My mother's womb? Isn't the womb meant to be the most comfortable place? Why does it burn so much?'*

'You were born from the fire of your father's wrath. The burning is the insult, kindled by his childhood friend, Dronacharya. To avenge himself, your father performed a fire sacrifice. When the manic flames blazed across the sky, he sacrificed into your mother his toxic masculine juice burdened with the load of humiliation. From that fire, you and your brother were born.'

I held myself with both my hands. Was this why I was 'Krishnaa'? Was my skin affected by the flames during my birth? My complexion was darker than others' and envied by people from lands I hadn't heard of. The black smoke didn't bother me any further.

The music of the flute fondled the notes of a monsoon raga, melodious but haunting. What was Father doing in the dark? Why did he sit there, leaning on my side of the empty bed? I asked no one. Enveloped within his melancholy, he was too distant to experience my dormant presence in his locus.

'Drona's betrayal was devastating.' He closed his palm into a fist and hit the ground.

The betrayal of Dronacharya? The royal guru at Hastinapur generously slandered my father, proclaiming the opposite.

'Agreed, we were great friends when we were students at the ashram of Rishi Bhardwaj. But friendship is for equals. In those days, when we were both at the gurukul, we were equal. He excelled at defence, I at law and finance. I promised to share my kingdom with him. Later, when he came to me begging for help, we were no longer equals.'

Why? What was the clash? The question was obvious.

'He was destitute, and I was a king,' Father sneered. 'He had insulted his education and talent with his negligence. He embraced a life of extreme poverty, his endeavours anything but enterprising. How could I share my glory, my identity – my Panchal – with a man who could reduce the country to his state of penury? How could someone, who had failed to take care of his own family in spite of his incomparable power, bring development to an entire country?' King

Dhrupad's anger raised another cloud of black smoke.

'I showed the door to Drona. I wanted him to come back armed with his achievements, elevated from his state of suffering. I wanted him to return as my equal. He didn't understand this language of friendship. He wanted favours. A king never accepts favours. The very expectation made Drona incompetent to rule half the country.'

I had detested the man named Dronacharya, even before meeting him. Now, I abhorred him.

'As a king, it is my dharma to act for the welfare of my subjects. A meek, diffident Drona would have made a disastrous leader.' Father's long, deep sigh resonated with the burning smell of agony. 'He came back with Arjun as his one-man army to dethrone me. I would have willingly given him the other half of Panchal, if he had approached me as the rajguru of Hastinapur! I did not betray Drona, he betrayed me.'

Can't Father forgive him? For peace? My anxious appeal hung in the air. Father shook his head vigorously.

'I can't forgive him. In a king's world, such forgiveness gets recorded as timidity. It sets the wrong example.' Father Dhrupad observed the oak tree, blemished with a column of ugly holes on its branches. 'I have to prove to my subjects that I deserve to be their ruler not by the decree of my royal birth but by my leadership. Drona acquired what wasn't his by treachery. It was unlawful.'

What would all these lead to? My mind was sullen.

'One sin leads to another. History will accuse Drona of dismal failure. A failed man, who couldn't sustain a fair life. A failed friend, calculating charitable returns. A failed teacher, who exploited his student to pursue his vendetta.' He paused, as if to fathom the truth of his life wherein the past hurt and the future was blurry.

'In many parts of the world, the pot of adharma is brimming,' he resumed. 'When it overflows, there will be the greatest war of this era. It will not leave a single kingdom unscathed. Draupadi, my daughter, is destined to be the holy fuel in the war of dharma, where the biggest warriors will find themselves on opposite sides with the earth divided by the line of justice. And there will be destruction.'

Why does destruction lure so much? I shivered, not with fear but with a strange excitement, illogical, but distinct in my veins.

'The destruction will lead to a closure,' I heard the king say sadly. 'I will perish, and so will Drona. The next generation will take over. Drishtadyumn, Draupadi, Shikhandini, Arjun ...'

Why Arjun? How did his rage for Dronacharya not spill over to Arjun?

'Arjun was only the means to an end, fulfilling a task assigned to him by his teacher. He was neither the cause of the feud, nor its consequence,' Father continued calmly. 'Drona misused his relationships twice, with me and with Arjun. He has opened doors for the same manipulations to boomerang upon him ruthlessly. The teacher and the student will find themselves at war, not as allies but as opponents.'

The oak tree had crumpled: its trunk was bent lifelessly. The woodpecker flew away. Royal attendants left bowls full of jasmine flowers at regular intervals in the corridor. Chants of the priests floated in, praying for people and peace. Folding his hands and with eyes closed, Father joined the prayers.

'God!' he appealed. 'May the battles of my children be restricted within their own peripheries. Else yet another generation will be forced to engage with conflicts borne from the past, without a complete understanding of why they are important.'

Bells from the temple had started ringing. I wished I could make my presence felt. Father opened his eyes and closed again. 'May my children be empowered to be rid of all their blemishes during their lifetime.'

*

I hadn't realized when Krishna's flute had started moving swiftly through the cryptic beats of the monsoon raga, mischievously threatening to divert from the binding notes yet never falling off the edge. It was my signal to return. I drifted away, following the same melodious path that had taken me back in time.

3

Drops of water splashed on my face. I sat up startled. The Dvaita forest was dark, and everyone was still asleep. Only one bed was abandoned. High above, an arrow hung loosely from the tree trunk. It had ruptured the bark over the hollow that might have stored some rainwater. I clenched my teeth. There was no point chasing the miscreant. He would be far away by now on some expedition best known to himself.

Each time he left in the middle of the night, he'd employ mean tricks to wake me up. Hidden nuts of squirrels dropped on my belly. Creepers wrapped around my wrist and pulled awkwardly. Ripe berries fell into my open mouth; I got up choking.

I didn't have to do much to strike back. Maybe soil his quiver. Nothing irritated Arjun more than anyone touching his weapons casually. Or greasing his clothes, which he'd notice only when Mother Kunti called out sharply, and the brothers laughed at Mother's favourite being awarded an earful.

Left idle in the dark hours, I loitered around. Less than a mile away, the forest ground was carpeted by tiny red fruits. The night breeze was reckless, the tree generous. I picked up as much as I could in the corner of my cloth. The eastern sky was clearing up. From afar, I could see Mother Kunti getting ready for the daily chores after her morning meditation. Sahadev had collected logs for firewood, and Bhim had washed the grains to be boiled. Yudhishthir had cleared away the stray leaves while brainstorming with her the way out from some tedious obstacle. Nakul was cleaning a pot with many marks on it, joking that the scars on its shining surface were indicative of the glorious life of blessed princes who spent most of their time away from the throne. Mother

Kunti cast a disgruntled look at him. Others murmured something about not voicing bitter truths. I walked into this pleasant family banter, burying my displeasure towards the woman who had obligated me to marry five men.

I held towards her all the fruits I had picked from the forest. Mother Kunti silently stared at my palms with a strange expression. She touched the fruits and then my hand affectionately. Slowly, she looked up, only to step behind, shocked. Surprised at her odd response, I stayed pinned to my place, wondering if I should dump the fruits on the ground. She took a while to come forward and spread her cloth, into which I gently deposited my gatherings.

'I thought Madri is back. She used to bring me such gifts; her touch made the mundane precious.' She smiled, her eyes fixed on her lap.

'Madri! The other wife of Father Pandu?'

How could my mother-in-law be so cordial about this relationship!

A recent memory flashed in my mind. When I left Panchal with Arjun, Father Dhrupad had sent lavish presents – heavily embroidered fabrics, elaborate earthenware, spices and fresh vegetables, gold and silver. Many wars of our kingdom had been fought because the invaders wanted to get their hands on the rich artisanship and fertile soil of Panchal. The wares lay neglected before my new mother-in-law. 'We are poor forest dwellers. Expensive offerings will only attract us more enemies. Take them back with you, prince,' she told my brother. 'What is invaluable to us is with us already. We are grateful and delighted.'

Obediently, Brother Drishtadyumn bowed and made an exit.

Today, I watched Kunti hold the little red fruits I had picked from the forest like treasure. Her eyes fell on mine like a swift arrow, just stopping short of piercing its target. 'Yes, she was the co-wife. King Pandu's other wife.'

By then the brothers had dispersed. Was the lady really bizarre? Or did she enjoy harassing others? The concept of love was muddled in her head. Neither did she feel possessive about her husband, nor did she understand my need to possess mine!

My face may have conveyed to Mother Kunti what my words couldn't. 'The forest is beautiful, Draupadi. If you aren't capable of maintaining it, then it is better to delegate the responsibility to someone more qualified. Else, you will have to live with the burden of mismanagement.' Perhaps she was talking about herself, but I felt the words were pointed at me.

'I am a lot more capable than what is estimated of me. I prefer to be left on my own,' I retorted and turned to leave.

'Sit down.' The cold voice hit my spine. Authoritative and hypnotic. I did as she said, expecting her to spoil my day. What would she do to punish me? Would she hand over her chores to me and top them with extra work? Well, not a problem. I was immensely fond of making a home, arranging and rearranging things to change its look from time to time. Or would she invite all the beings of the forest for a feast and ask me to cook up a meal? That too would be child's play. I loved to cook, eat and feed – experimenting with spices and ingredients. I chuckled internally, while maintaining a serious face on the fore.

Mother Kunti wasn't offended, though I had given her enough reason. She didn't ask for anything I had expected. Instead, she told me about her days with Madri, the mother of Nakul and Sahadev, and her beauty, talent and immense love for Father Pandu. She sat in silence afterwards, reminiscing about the past and reliving her own youth, severed from the usual human desires.

'Co-wives are like perks that come with leadership acquisitions. You have to negotiate the terms tactfully so that they don't threaten your bliss.' Her advice baffled me again.

'Co-wives! You mean I will have co-wives too?' I almost screamed.

'Bhim is already married to Hidimbi, a dweller of the Kamyak forest.' She would have said more about Hidimbi too, had I not raised my hand with absolute disinterest.

'I mean Arjun.'

Mother Kunti sighed. 'How would I know?' She looked at me, sad and amused at the same time. 'Politics is a tough game. Every relationship operates as a function of the society. Nothing and no one is personal.'

'I know what a palace with a courtroom looks like. I was born and brought up in those corridors,' I gasped. 'Royalty is no excuse to philander. Unless the matriarch prefers divisive politics.' Angry tears filled my eyes. 'I wouldn't allow a co-wife anywhere close to my existence.'

Mother Kunti touched my hand gently. I pulled it away. 'I hope you are able to stick by that decision if at all such a situation arises.' she said. 'For now, let me share with you some of the lessons I have learnt over a lifetime. They will help you sail through tough waters.'

Mother Kunti forced me to match steps with her, teaching self-defence and martial skills. She was a strict teacher, impatient with failures and more ecstatic than I for each correct move. Sometimes she invited Bhim and Arjun to join us for fist fighting and archery. I was a lousy student, more interested in keeping the house and whipping up a delicious meal. My offerings evoked voracious praise from Bhim, but the mother-in-law had a worse appetite than a sparrow.

'Couldn't your father at least train you to hold the sword? What on earth were you doing all through your childhood?' she would reprimand me.

'Patience, Mother,' Yudhishthir would intervene.

In my leisure hours, I was out there befriending the bounteous world, consumed in the glorious sunset by the riverside. The colours dancing on the water made every evening festive. I sat there and wove garlands with pink and white flowers, none of which I carried back. At night, when the men returned, I sometimes found the garlands entwined around Arjun's wrist. The day for forest dwellers started way earlier than the rest of the earth. There was less haste, more happiness, more spontaneity and fewer protocols. I distributed tiny morsels from our food amongst the squirrels and birds. Mother Kunti wasn't impressed by any of these virtues. She kept a distance, observing everything with acute alertness as though one moment of inattention would lead to disaster.

✱

'Krishna, was she always such a grumpy, dispassionate woman?'

'No, Krishnaa, life makes her seem so. She has been truly fond of only two women. One was Madri, the other is you.'

'Me! Her fondness threw me before five pairs of eyes and hands. Even an enemy wouldn't do that. The relationship with one's mother-in-law is always filled with thorns!'

'Talk to her, Krishnaa. Seek your answers. She is willing to give you everything. But much to her disappointment, you are not asking.'

✱

I was tracing the chakor one of those days, the cloth on my body hanging clumsily, my limbs lazy and hair looking dishevelled. Mother Kunti came flying towards me, discontent bursting from her eyes. She held my hand roughly, pulling me towards a secluded corner in the forest. How much she hated indiscipline! As I watched awestruck, she climbed up a tree swiftly, pulled out a little pot from a hole in the trunk and jumped down to land perfectly on the ground. I rushed to help her, thinking she might need a foot massage. Pushing me away with a grimace, she turned me around and tapped my shoulder, prompting me to sit. Grumbling all the while about my atrocious habits, she applied the liquid from the pot she had brought down with her. It poured on the crown of my head and trickled down. Kunti deftly arrested its freedom, forcing the liquid through the strands the way she wanted. My defiant hair was tamed between her fingers. She tied it up into a tight braid, leaving not one strand out of place.

I almost chuckled as she continued to complain. She caught me doing that.

'How difficult was it, Mother, to parent and protect five boys all by yourself?'

I didn't ask this!

I wasn't even thinking about it. Krishna played these pranks, unexpectedly assuming my voice and preponing a conversation before I was ready. I didn't call him a conspirator just because I loved the word.

Tightened jaws relaxed. 'It was eventful. We are blessed with deep scars that gallant warriors flaunt like trophies.' she said. 'They left thrilling memories and armed us with a never-resting reflex.' Mother Kunti spoke without regrets sitting by my side.

A heart cast in iron with the skin of a human – did this fall under a defined sub-sect of human beings?

'What am I supposed to do with the five brothers as husbands? Why did you do this?' I asked finally, baring the anguish in my heart.

The chakor had finished its songs and disappeared to another destination. The rustle of the fallen leaves reminded that those too could fly. Mother Kunti spent some moments in silence, as if gauging the character of the hour. Satisfied by the absence of a third party in audience, she looked as if she had been waiting for this question.

'It is the ritual of the country to pass on the most priceless possession to a deserving successor. This is what Indra willed; Krishna too.' She smiled.

Krishna! Krishna willed? I clutched a clod of dry earth beneath my palm; it broke into dust. Picking up my agitated hand, Mother Kunti placed it inside hers. We hadn't realized when the summer sun had gone behind the dark clouds. Water droplets dripped down our skin; the ants and reptiles slothing around rushed into their burrows. The rains didn't take much time to catch up. I sprang to my feet, hoping we'd run for shelter. When she showed no haste for reposition,

I gladly sat back at my place. On the other side, Mother Kunti's pristine white attire, now wet, clung transparently to her body. She closed her eyes and tipped her face towards the sky, as if she was being kissed by the downpour. The radiance on her face was unmissable.

'For the world, they are five different beings visible in five different bodies, Draupadi. In reality, they are one.' Her voice was submerged in the rhythm of the rain as if each note was being thoughtfully aligned. I wondered whether this was the inebriation of a lost woman drunk in nature's fervent intoxicant. Sublime happiness shone in her eyes; it could transform a thousand pots of poison into the nectar of immortality. This godly beauty couldn't be a deception. I couldn't take my eyes off.

'The boys are Indra's illusion.' The voice sparked again, as the showers heaved upon us forcefully. 'Five different manifestations for five distinct sets of virtues that are too conflicting for one body to host together. One of them acts as the central system for the others facing the four directions of the world. Explore for yourself, Draupadi. As a wedding gift, your poor, jungle-dwelling mother-in-law has given you the entire Maha Bharat!'

4

At Hastinapur, the Kaurav celebrated the death of their Pandav cousins, having plotted to burn them alive in the *Lakshyagriha* of Varnavrat, built especially for the purpose with highly inflammable material. Certain death was avoided due to the intervention of Uncle Vidur. He warned Mother Kunti of the Kaurav conspiracy in advance. They all escaped through a secret tunnel and were ferried across the river Ganga. Charred corpses of a tribal woman and her sons at the *Lakshyagriha* were mistaken as those of the Pandav family. Uncle Dhritarashta, the Kaurav monarch, addressed his nation with a speech mourning for the souls of his dead relatives, praying for them to be happily united with their father, Pandu, in heaven.

'Who were these five men and the lady?' I interrupted Nakul, wondering how the numbers matched perfectly between the alive and the dead.

Nakul hesitated, leaving nothing to the imagination. 'Hoaxing the Kaurav was necessary. Mother Kunti needed time to think.'

I was aghast.

Edging the banks of the Saraswati river, towards the west of Hastinapur, was the Kamyak forest. The birds there sang hymns of forgiveness and the poetry of desolation. Flocks of deer leaped around. The Pandav would wash their faces in the crystal-clear riverwater and rest under the shades of tall trees. They also fended off the attacks of Rakshas clans and accepted invitations from ascetics. Once their resentful heads were sufficiently calm, they decided to wait for a strategic confrontation when the time was right, instead of retaliating in haste.

'Mother Kunti started preparing us for a battle against the establishment,' Nakul said.

'We were not the establishment. It was about time we accepted it,' he added, quoting her. 'Battles require blessings, allies and experience. She instructed Bhim to begin a rigorous training for himself and the others. Arjun was to be in constant touch with Krishna.'

Soon after my marriage, we all went back to Hastinapur. We were received with tears of joy by King Dhritarashtra and Queen Gandhari. The queen had wrapped a piece of cloth around her eyes since the time she had married her visually impaired husband. The gesture raised grounds for detailed analysis in every region of the country. Each mouth had an opinion. I spared myself the pain of adding to the pool and touched her feet. She felt the contours of my face with her hand, 'The fame of Draupadi's beauty travels everywhere in the country. I am sure what my palms touched is splendid.' She kissed my forehead. 'I am more enamoured with what her presence makes me feel. This fossil of a palace is suddenly breathing again.'

Her love was gratifying. And the grand, old

palace was indeed intimidating. As if clandestine sacrilege was buried between the substructures – they seized from the royal inhabitants their freedom to pursue happiness or express sadness. Anger was in the air, a loud laughter garnered glances of disapproval. Days were methodical here – time-bound and rigid with etiquettes.

*

'Krishna, why has everyone here made peace with the discomfort?'

'Because questioning the discomfort would invite greater discomforts, Krishnaa.'

'Is there any one source from where I may begin?'

'Sources are rare. Onlookers are opinionated. Most of those who contributed to the history are dead.'

'Not all are dead, Krishna. I know whom to approach.'

*

Born as Prince Devavrat to King Shantanu and Ganga, the man had sacrificed the throne for his stepbrothers and taken a grand oath of celibacy so his progeny would not seek any rights either. The gods came together to shower their blessings on him and honour such a selfless gesture. Since then, he had been titled Bhishma, the tremendous, leaving his mark in history not as a king but as a kingmaker.

Secluded by steep, tall walls that kept intruders at bay, Bhishma came across as a fierce workaholic when I met him for the first time. After the customary blessings, he cast a sharp, disgruntled look at Mother Kunti and walked away. The white hair, fine lines around the eyes and wrinkled skin couldn't conceal how incredibly handsome he was. With his head held high, he towered over Arjun and walked faster than any of the Kaurav or Pandav brothers. I kept looking back to observe Bhishma marching away. He looked diagonally where greedy birds were fighting over scattered grains. They fluttered their wings and fled. An attendant rushed in to scoop the grains from the porch.

We met King Dhritarashtra's half-brother, Vidur, on the balcony, who said I looked like Goddess Lakshmi. I gazed downwards; Bhishma had stopped to talk to Bhim. I couldn't hear what they were discussing. Bhim followed him to the other end of the vestibule. The granduncle was patting his back for accomplishments that mattered. Wherever I was escorted in the Hastinapur palace, whomever I met, whatever ritual I participated in, one part of my mind kept in touch with Bhishma.

A few days after, when everyone was resting in their own chambers, I ran through the corridors towards the oldest door in the palace. It was gleaming like it had just been erected. I knocked.

'Who is there?' the voice roared from inside, irritated by the unhesitant interruption into his few hours of privacy.

'Open the door,' I called out.

The door flung open. Before me stood the astonished legend, wondering if he was hallucinating or if the new bride was indeed a lunatic. I stepped in boisterously through the entrance, without waiting for permission. With hands on his waist, he frowned. 'What can I do for you?'

A relentless machine running steadily for years had just confronted an undue halt. The displeasure showed. He was extremely irked with the liberties I was taking. Violation of decorum was a punishable offence.

'We need to talk,' I said cheerfully, unwilling to notice the unwelcoming reception. I had no clue what I would talk about. Reaching the edge of his patience, his cold gaze drilled into me like a scholar would despise a chattering crow. I gawked around at this museum of a chamber with minimal amenities, known and unknown histories deposited in its vaults over the centuries. Bhishma impatiently cleared his throat from behind.

'Why is it so claustrophobic here?' I looked around, ignoring the signal.

Bhishma's abode had three windows in three different directions, opening towards the martial training centre, the armoury and the treasury. The three regal buildings peaked into the sky, blocking the sunlight with their expansion. At the other end, one window was closed. I moved towards it. Bhishma desperately looked for words to throw me out. Dealing with his grand daughter-in-law was a skill he was yet to master.

'I have business to attend,' he declared angrily.

'Why is this shut, Granduncle?' I asked, strolling ahead leisurely, and unbolted the rusty lock of the huge casement.

An unexplained horror swept across his face. He rushed forward to stop me.

Insurgent breeze charged in like me, without waiting for the great man's consent. On the other side, life bustled in colours and flavours: grazing goats and thundering clouds, singing birds and passing travellers sharing stories of other lands. He commanded me to seal the window back right away. I didn't answer him or follow his instruction.

'We have been taught lessons about the great Bhishma, one of the most illustrious politicians of the country. Since then, I have been wondering how he looks, what he sounds like, where he dwells ...' My flattery fell flat.

'Have you been taught to be disobedient, too?' he said with tremendous ire. 'Do as I said. And leave these chambers alone.'

The stuffiness was cleaning up slowly with the fresh air entering from outside, unburdened with calls of duty. The gigantic chamber seemed to be breathing after years of compromised ventilation. The change in energy was therapeutic. Outside the window, urchins attempted to pluck mangoes from large trees. Fishermen rejoiced ferrying their trade to the other side of the river. The mayhem of existence was apparent, bustling with noise and smell, leaving a touch of life in Bhishma's abode. Yet, the elderly man wasn't touched by this mirth. He speeded towards the window to close it himself.

'Please don't,' I pleaded. 'Even if for a brief while, let it stay open.'

Something in my voice made him stop. He still looked offended, but his demeanour softened. I sat down on the floor to touch his feet and seek his blessing. He didn't stop me, but did not bless me either.

'Why are you here?' he asked again. He had calmed down considerably, and his resistance had subsided. He looked at the window – with hesitation – as if he wanted to stay aloof but couldn't take his eyes off.

'Everyone knows everything about Bhishma,' I whispered. 'I want to know about Devavrat. Tell me about the forgotten prince.'

Bhishma staggered back, stunned and daunted by my insistence. 'You haven't been taught diplomacy either,' he muttered gravely.

Courtesy be damned, I rebelled further from the royal formalities. 'A lot about Hastinapur lies buried in the remoulding of Devavrat into Bhishma. I am searching for the remains of that youth, whose transition is celebrated but his past is disowned. Is it a crime to ask this question?'

I saw a glint in the eyes of the granduncle. 'What will you do with the information?' he asked softly.

'All that I know is significant, but not complete. I want to take pride in the history of my matrimonial family. Bhishma's neglected past leaves a gap in the chronological restructuring of the present. I am only trying to join the dots.'

Bhishma stared at me for a brief while, which felt like hours. 'Every generation in this palace has been touched by ambitious reformers. Mother Ganga, Stepmother Satyavati. Then came Amba,' he paused, seeming somewhat stressed. 'Your Mother-in-law Kunti, and now you.' He smiled finally. 'The men of this house are no more than puppets before the will of the women. That is a truth I usually don't confess.' He lowered his voice, bending towards me. 'Bhishma is no legendary politician, only a royal servant with principles.'

He sat down on his wooden bed that was covered with a simple cotton sheet, without even a pillow to rest his head.

The floodgates had opened.

I took his leave and went back to visit him after a few days. The fourth window was still open. He hadn't shut it. Dewdrops washed the barren windowsill, birds perching to rest from the rains. He had made peace with them. I looked at him happily.

'The window you opened has a large mahogany frame on which Devavrat once sat listening to the pulse of nature. The youthful days of romance and adventure, once lost, cannot be recovered. Close the window, Panchali. I haven't done it to honour your spirit. These winds make me weak. I am trained to match my instincts with the trumpet of elephants and the clang of a sword striking a warrior's shield. Devavrat died a long time back. The dead can be revived only as ghosts. It is inauspicious. Close it.'

I didn't move. With great affection, I persuaded the grand uncle to reclaim his past. In acknowledgment of the love he seldom received, he took small steps forward to join a stubborn woman two generations down in the family hierarchy. I took his feet on my lap, as he sat on the other end of the window to support his back. Gently, I ran my fingers over the scars and bulging veins that spoke of recondite lore across the years.

'Devavrat isn't dead, Granduncle. He lies

dormant in you,' I spoke as softly as I could. Even the passing wind couldn't hear the words that were preserved for preferred audience. 'Killing one who desired to live is a bigger sin than all the accolades resulting from a grand oath. When you are with me, be Devavrat. For one person in this house, may I exist not just as Arjun's wife but also as Draupadi.'

*

The world recognized Bhishma for his might. In the little time we had for ourselves, I witnessed Devavrat's disquiet, concealed behind years of suppression. I wiped the tears that had not flown in decades. I held his hands firmly on that day when the Pandav were tossed out of their ancestral house. He shivered with a high fever but had not allowed another soul to know about it. Bhishma's hands were figuratively tied to serve the throne, no matter who sat on it. Gracing the throne was King Dhritarashtra, blind in sight and also in wisdom. Also blinded by paternal love, he had allowed his son Duryodhan to play with the kingdom. No advice, no reprimands worked with the impaired and the greedy.

On that ceremonious morning, King Dhritarashtra called for an announcement with the Pandav and the Kaurav standing behind him. 'My beloved brother Pandu appeared in my dreams last night. Our childhood banter which—' his voice choked. Aunt-in-law Gandhari nudged him from behind, urging him to stick to the point. Irritated, he began again, this time sticking to the script. 'Pandu's sons are strong and able, as are my own. Now I must put the young men in charge and relax.' He smiled a little too much. When no one reciprocated, he added that Hastinapur was to remain with the Kaurav while the menacing forest of Khandav would henceforth become the kingdom of the Pandav.

A sudden hush followed, with only the Kaurav cheering. Yudhishthir folded his hands to seek blessings of the elders for a new beginning. Arjun volunteered to reach the site first. Krishna accompanied him like he always did. Khandav forest was uprooted in no time. The beautiful city of Indraprastha was set up in its place.

5

Bhishma sat down with the council to get the agreements signed and the treaty announced. He held meetings between the Pandav and Kaurav – jointly and separately – to explain the details of the estate and discuss its economics. He set up a new council of ministers for the Pandav and trained them for hours at end on politics and developmental planning. I saw very little of him until one evening on my way back from the temple with Aunt Gandhari and Mother Kunti, when I noticed him stationed on the southern window. My mother-in-law was walking stone-faced, in contrast to Queen Gandhari, who was issuing constant instructions to her attendants on trivial matters. Without a word, I slipped away from the depressing company. Bhishma turned to see me standing behind him and looked back at the greenery outside. Shades of the dusk had begun colouring the horizon.

'This window,' he revealed, 'I closed it the day I became Bhishma.'

It would be a long and difficult evening. I sat down on the corner of his bed.

'Having grown up in a famous father's diligent care, I didn't have many reasons to miss my mother. I still loved going back to her from time to time. This window opens towards her. Listen closely, you will feel her too.' Childlike glee overcame him. Indeed we could hear the burbling of the river, flowing in vigour like an eager mother in her youth, caught up in myriad chores while singing a lullaby to her child. The river Ganga.

On the exterior wall around the window, a *madhavi lata* spiralled upwards, its red flowers in full bloom and vibrant leaves spread wide. Dozens of butterflies flocked around it, the colours on their wings tuning the melody of love in the wake of spring. 'Child Devavrat would imagine the wild emerging from the green camouflage of the madhavi lata, attempting to launch an unexpected attack on him and his father, which he'd dismiss with his toy sword.'

Had anyone seen this divine smile on the face of Bhishma? He had grown a few years younger. He looked less like a veteran and more like a friend.

'As he grew taller, his dreams grew bigger. Now Devavrat had started thinking of the country and the world, his relationships in it and—' he hesitated before blurting out, 'Women!'

*

'Bhishma is barbaric, a demon in disguise. He is a pervert. The world knows very little about him. He should be stabbed with a thousand arrows.' Shikhandini had exploded once after Father had filled us in on the brave expeditions of Bhishma.

'How do you know?' I felt hurt. I had been looking forward to know more while studying the politics of Maha Bharat. Bhishma was my hero. Shikhandini didn't care to explain.

That was many summers ago, in Panchal. Why did I remember this now? I tried to shake it off my head.

*

'In a palace that prides on its kings flaunting many marriages, didn't Devavrat ever fall in love?' I tried to make it easier for the old man. Used to my shameless peeks into his life by now, Bhishma laughed out loud. To me, it sounded like tears. 'Devavrat's entitlements were lost even before he had grown up enough to ask that question to himself.'

'Still,' I whispered, unwilling to give up. Unwilling to believe that a fine prince with outstanding credentials had never experienced love.

'No!' Bhishma shook his head forcefully. But I feel responsible for Amba. She was a magnificent woman with dreams of her own.' He was lost in nostalgia, perhaps immersed in self-pity too. 'When I abducted the three princesses of Kashi from their swayamvar upon the instructions of Mother Satyavati, I didn't look at my prisoners. They were meant to be wed to my half-brother Vichitravirya. Things changed quickly thereafter.' He heaved a sigh. 'Amba, the eldest sister, was in love with Salva, the king of Saubala, whom I had defeated when he came to rescue the girls. Once informed, I charioted her back to Salva. He refused to accept her because he hadn't been able to protect her from her abductor. Vanity is the pride of the incapable.'

Bhishma stopped abruptly, his voice quivering. His fingers, locked into a fist, opened suddenly as he resumed, 'Amba was heartbroken. She returned with hatred in her eyes and vengeance in her heart. That was when I noticed her. Beautiful and fierce, demanding to marry me. Demanding to transform my life into the same hell I had turned hers. I lost the voice and power to object when she blamed me for Salva's failings in love.'

The elderly man looked outside the window again, his silver hair being caressed by the breeze. 'I was astounded by her words.' He closed his eyes. 'Her beauty too, if I may confess. I refused to defend myself.'

'Why?' I was feeling restless inside.

Bhishma took a deep breath. 'If you can't improve a situation, then the biggest comfort you can offer to the agonized is to be the one she can blame. An unidentified enemy is frustrating. And I was her legitimate culprit.' Bhishma touched the windowpane with the back of his palm. 'Amba cursed amid a gathering of ministers and associates that time would turn and she would bring upon me a horrible death.'

I shuddered and inched closer to the old man, waiting to be told that such threats didn't bother him. But Bhishma had shed his guard.

'Amba gave up her life. On that unfortunate morning, behind closed doors, Devavrat was awake. The eyes accustomed to weigh people by their purpose were misty. Devavrat promised to the soul of Amba that whenever she would return to avenge her misfortune, Bhishma would neither stop nor fight her.'

'What are you saying, Granduncle?' I spoke furiously. 'You shouldn't have abducted the princesses. Why didn't you refuse Mother Satyavati's command?' I felt conflicted. Father had never told us about this story.

'Bhishma is barbaric, a demon in disguise. He is a pervert.' Shikhandini's words that had hurt me then felt even more hurtful now.

'I have pledged loyalty to the throne, and Mother Satyavati was the reigning queen,' Bhishma defended. Devavrat lamented.

'You hadn't pledged your conscience,' I insisted.

'I am supposed to solve all problems of the royalty. Conscience itself can be a problem sometimes,' he philosophized.

We stared at each other without a word. Bhishma may have imprisoned Amba during her life, but, with her death, Amba had erected an everlasting cage entrapping Bhishma. My hands were too short to pull the old man out of this unyielding enclosure.

'No one can harm you, history can attest that. You should stop thinking about Amba.' When logic fails, denial helps. Somewhere deep within, I was getting protective towards this wonderful, elderly man. He was suffering in isolation. Wasn't that enough punishment?

He placed a hand on my head, blessing me. 'Amba is there somewhere, reborn in the same world, still suffering the agony of her earlier life. She will launch her deadly attack, towing behind the one I have loved the most.'

'Who?'

I screamed, determined to face the sword of Amba and her companion should they attempt to eliminate my granduncle. Startled by the outburst, he drew me closer and kissed my forehead.

'Who?' I asked again.

'Devavrat,' he smiled. 'Amba will unite with Devavrat one day. Together, they will conspire and put an end to Bhishma.'

He was lying. He didn't want to tell me the name. Devavrat was gone, Bhishma was back. I got up and left.

*

'Krishna, is Granduncle Bhishma barbaric? Is he a pervert?'

'What does your heart tell you, Krishnaa? The heart never lies.'

'My heart says he is godly. Shikhandini says he is demonic.'

'Then he is demonic and a pervert for Shikhandini. For you, he is godly. Why do you confuse yourself?'

*

Before the war of Kurukshetra, the nights descended into unbearable silence. The pretence of the apparent calm was palpable. Each house in the country had signed off its energies, the people resting their throbbing hearts under blankets.

None could shut their eyes, lest an unpleasant dream found its way. Everyone clutched onto their dear ones – waiting with dread for the nightmare in the morning – for no one knew which moment would be their last. The weary sighs of the army wives spiralled up in the air. Their husbands held on to the families, quietly counting the hours. Amidst such uncertainty, I heard the ghosts of Khandavprastha raising their heads after years of lying comatose, now contemplating a partnership with the Evil.

That evening I visited Mother Kunti. She was sitting outside her tent, her forehead, as usual, wrinkled with difficult ruminations. With a forefinger, she made odd symbols on the soil. Something about them was not as per her liking. She cleared everything with an agitated hand and restarted. She looked skywards with frantic eyes and found me waiting.

'The galaxies are more truthful than humans, more straightforward than destiny,' she said when I asked. She seemed lost in helpless grief, praying for mercy and kindness. Wasn't she happy that the great battle of Kurukshetra was about to commence? Was she mourning the inevitable end of the Evil? Had she forgiven? Many questions clouded my mind.

'I have far more to lose in this battle of Dharma than anyone can gain,' she said, melancholy dripping from every word.

She looked at me the same way as when I had first met her – with great affection and greater expectations. And she asked the unthinkable: 'Draupadi, why did you stop Anga Raj from participating in your swayamvar? Wasn't he as worthy as Arjun?'

A mother-in-law querying why the woman married to her sons had refused to be someone else's wife was unsettling. I didn't know how to respond. How fair was it to bring up those memories? But such was Mother Kunti – capable of initiating any discourse if she felt her ask was valid. So what if the customary world found them unacceptable.

God knows what prompted her strange obsession with my personal life! Especially the part of my life which was routed through my heart.

> *'I wanted a visionary as my husband, Mother. Karn would have capsuled me within the shells of silly social bindings, just like he allowed his valour to be enveloped by the undeserving.'*

Again, these were not my words. Krishna had spoken on my behalf. I couldn't push him away because he wasn't anywhere near me.

*

Father Dhrupad did not want a simple swayamvar for his beloved daughter. He called for a grand ceremony. Shikhandini deftly assumed charge of the arrangements and retired him to fulfil other kingly duties. What was on her mind, she told nobody. In the decided month, lavish tents in bright colours cropped up on the palace premises. The beds inside were covered with soft velvet. The first ray of the moon pierced through gold-bordered windows. All attendee kings were welcomed with beautiful cane baskets packed with honey, coconuts, spices, fruits, *resham*, a sword of silver and a beautiful gold emblem of Panchal. Lotus water was sprinkled on the guests before they were ushered to their tents by attendants trained to offer soothing body massages as proficiently as they discussed geography, agriculture, pottery and goldmining. The morning breeze greeted them with the blessings of the Ganga. Before the princes could make their wishes known, horses and palanquins were at the doorsteps to ferry them for a holy bath. Panchal was adorned with huge lanterns hanging from tree branches. Earthen lamps lined even the most desolate streets. Conferences were held over the next few days on topics ranging from warfare to administration, trade laws to book-keeping. Word spread faster than the speed of light. We were soon joined by the Devas and Gandharvas, the Asurs and Brahmins, all seeking to participate in the great swayamvar. Everyone was received with equal warmth.

One night, I forced Shikhandini to go to bed earlier than usual. She looked unwell. 'When did you manage to organize so much?' I asked. She pointed to her aching forehead. It was a command for me to nurse her with a firm massage. 'Why do you overexert? Can't you just sit back and rest?'

She turned to the other side and slept off.

The carnival left everyone singing ballads about the beauty, creativity and opulence of Panchal. On the final day, however, the warriors were stumped. Shikhandini had planted a seemingly impossible competition in the experience of any human or celestial warrior. Even Father Dhrupad and Drishtadyumn were looking around awkwardly.

The participants had to look into the water reflection on the ground and target the eye of a fish hanging on top, swaying rigorously in the air. The water below was ridged with ripples, disturbing the already unsteady image. Many of the princes in the gathering stepped back, unwilling to embrace certain failure. Those who went ahead, abused my father for inviting the greatest warriors of the lands only to insult them amid public audience. King Dhrupad held a strict face. The gathering had started dispersing, as more and more kings made unsuccessful attempts.

'Is this a swayamvar or a farcical display of

forced affection towards an unplanned daughter?' someone shouted.

'The king seems to be searching for someone to exact vengeance against Dronacharya, on the pretext of seeking a daughter's suitor,' another echoed.

King Dhrupad laughed at them. 'The avenger of Drona lives inside my home.' He pointed at Drishtadyumn. 'Draupadi, my daughter, will marry the one who deserves her in appearance and mind, valour and spirit.'

When the gossip and debates were at their peak, in walked the *tejasvi*! Tall, muscular, handsome and confident, he lit up a thousand suns merely with his presence. A mesmerizing *kavach* shielded his chest and a pair of sparkling *kundals* hung from his ears. The hands vowed to lift mountains; his eyes shone like the blade of a sword. There was a calm detachment in his eyes. The kind of detachment that comes when one has fought with the world inch by inch, carving his own ecosystem by disowning the rest. He seemed like someone who didn't care to love or be loved. He was saintly, he also looked devilish. I shifted uncomfortably on my seat as he walked towards the stage.

This man wasn't my fantasy. His harsh languor proclaimed he'd fulfil all his duties but would remain grossly untouched by the songs of life. I looked restlessly at his progressing footsteps. The announcer in the hall was nervously shuffling away through the notes, unable to figure who this tejasvi was and where he had come from. My father's eyes met mine. Immediately, he asked the handsome man to stop, requesting for an introduction. Shikhandini leaped forward and blocked his way. Turning around now, his lips curved like a cruel critic.

'My work is my identity!' he pronounced, his voice falling against the walls and reverberating across the palace. 'I come from nowhere and belong to no one.'

He glared, waiting for something unpleasant to unfold. It did.

'A lack of belongingness is not the sign of a good upbringing, my son,' Father said. 'Even the great sacrificing sages assert with precious propitiation the identity of the clans they came from. What ideology runs in your blood? Which parents are you here to glorify? Tell us something about your lineage.'

The gathering had started murmuring by now.

'Anga Raj Karn,' someone mentioned.

'Born to mysterious parents, no one knows who,' said another.

'Brought up by Adhirath, a charioteer and his wife, Radha. A charioteer's son,' giggled another as someone hushed, 'Befriended and made the king of Anga by Duryodhan, the prince of Hastinapur.'

'Don't miss the *kavach* on his chest and the *kundal* in his ears,' yet another voice pointed out. 'The legend goes that Karn's kavach kundal can dilute Shiva's Pashupat. No weapon can have any effect on him while he wears them.'

'I have none to glorify.' The tejasvi gritted his teeth. 'I have only myself to represent. I came to the world with nothing and will depart empty-handed. This is the identity of every single person here, as is mine. This is who I choose to be, unlike others trapped in past accolades, flashing the illustrious ancestry they were fortunate to descend from. A family is not my identity. My brain and my strength are my credentials.' The sarcasm in his voice was visible now, paralleled with the striking face shining with unfamiliar luminance of inexplicable talent.

'Do you love Panchali?'

Shikhandini's blatant question fell on him like the stroke of a sword, cutting off his speech. Her directness in a public gathering ruffled the audience. The silence was deafening.

'Do you love Panchali?' she asked again.

'I don't know anything about her.' This time the tejasvi was more solemn. He made no attempts to look towards his left where I was seated. Shikhandini looked at Father Dhrupad like an artful lawyer, who had just killed the defence.

My father nodded sadly. 'Son, the strength of a man doesn't lie only in his arms. It is the strength of his personality that proves his might.'

Karn's eyes sharpened like the pointed end of

his arrows. His fingers tightened around his bow, itching to smash everything around him.

'The foster child of the charioteer Adhirath would be welcomed with open arms, had you not been so secretive about your invaluable parentage. Where is the pride of Radheya? Why would the son she nurtured with care, sharing home and wheat, be ashamed to celebrate her motherhood? Just because you have been mocked by the unsophisticated?'

King Dhrupad truly looked distraught as he reprimanded Karn, no different than when he scolded my brother every time he committed a folly.

'The world inflicts many cruel impositions on individuals. How you allow them to affect you is a test of your character. The arrogance of your bow you display in abundance and Radha's tenderness you so easily disown?' he paused, looking straight into the eyes of the meritorious youth, preparing to explain himself with regret but resolute firmness.

'You haven't come here for Draupadi. You are

here for yourself, to exhibit your prowess with the bow and establish a vain validation through this alliance. Maybe you will accomplish the swayamvar challenge. But I declare you ineligible to try. A father refuses to submit his daughter for the rehabilitation of a weak mind, which feels victimized despite receiving the best training in warfare from the great Guru Parashuram, the most devoted upbringing from a loving mother and a kingdom in lieu of his friendship with the prince of Hastinapur.'

The gathering watched with bated breath. The few warriors stood up immediately, picking their arms to gratify the tejasvi. A murmur of unrest spread. Karn lifted his hand and stopped them. Stepping forward towards King Dhrupad, he shivered with rage, his eyes seething with bitterness.

'Drown in your bottomless deficiencies, you and your daughters, who hide their prejudice behind pompous philosophy. Be prepared to suffer whatever comes as a consequence of this evening.' He left the stage, walking away with large steps, as every eye locked in on his erect spine from behind.

This wasn't a memory I was ready to negotiate, unless Mother Kunti brought me to face it. Krishna's response to her question had stiffened her. I touched her knee. 'Yes, Mother. Anga Raj was no match against Arjun then. Today, he is not even a comparison. They only have a few things in common – courage, rivalry and some common tastes maybe. Else, one supports the Evil, the other is in the company of the Divine. That makes all the difference.'

Mother Kunti pulled away.

6

I had crossed paths with Karn many times after – in the royal gardens of Hastinapur and in the palace corridors. I would see him walking by while I stood with Mother Kunti and Aunt-in-law Gandhari on the balcony. The elderly ladies would be discussing life, relationships and rituals when I would detect his energetic footsteps approaching us from behind. Karn would bow before the mothers with utmost respect and make a quick exit, leaving me alert and Mother Kunti speechless. While strolling around on idle afternoons, I'd observe mysterious shadows forming on my path from the kavach gleaming in placid sunlight and disappearing after a brief moment. He would even stop to play with my newborn sons, tickling their bellies as they laughed from someone else's lap. With me, he behaved as if I was invisible, just like he had done on the first day when we stood inside the palace of Panchal turned away from each other. I was alert whenever he was around and he, indifferent. We both knew neither of us had forgiven or forgotten.

He came to my swayamvar to win a coveted trophy. I ended up marrying his biggest rival. In his dismissal of me, he dismissed Arjun too. His resentment was revealed shamelessly many years after – when the bravest warriors of Hastinapur convened to vilify one solitary woman. Tejasvi Karn had heartily participated in the slandering, when he called me 'the woman of many men'. Mother Kunti was not ignorant of its implications.

I didn't realize when I had started breathing faster. Mother Kunti placed her cold hands on my blazing skin, caring enough to dilute the pain but manipulative enough to resist a recovery. She was a strange friend, who understood a lot without being told explicitly. She could also intimidate with her access to scandalous information from sources best known to herself.

'Why this question today, Mother?' I managed to ask.

'He is strong, handsome and known to possess a heart of gold. How did your feminine longing not notice him? I am curious.' She threw another sinful question at me without hesitation.

I got up to leave, wondering what stroke of senility had caused her to continue discussing another man with her daughter-in-law. Was she testing my integrity?

Kunti grabbed my hand with the desperation of a mother – a label that can force the wealthiest to behave like an impoverished. 'Draupadi, only Karn is capable of fighting Arjun and defeating him too. If there is ever a war between the two, only one will remain. And the war is only a few nights away.' Her voice choked, 'Do something, do anything. Stop them from fighting each other.' Her eyes filled with tears. She didn't try to hide them. A conjecture brewing inside my head was confirmed. This evening, Mother Kunti wasn't concerned about the safety of Arjun.

Was she expecting me to seduce Karn and destroy his resolve to fight Arjun? Of course, she was. My jaws pressed together. I loosened her hold over my hand and walked away with a heavy heart. She didn't stop me.

Below the open sky, I stopped to light a lamp before the tulsi plant. I bowed before it and turned towards my tent. Two army wives were waiting with news. 'Bhishma has decreed that Karn can't enter the battleground until he, the chief general of the Kaurav army, retains his position. Karn is livid, so is Duryodhan.'

Restless feet slowed down. What had led the old man to make such a controversial decision? I looked behind. Mother Kunti was still seated in the same position. With the sun retired for the day, I could vaguely see an outline of her. The woman knew how to get what she wanted. They said every hand of dice targeted one prime pawn but multiple collaterals were simultaneously readied for disposal. Did I really think I was her last resort?

Prosperous kingdoms with towering palaces boasted of impressive armouries. Arjun's collection was famous across all lands. His mother's weapons were even more deadly but known to none!

*

'Why are we here, Arjun?'

I had asked him on one of those late hours at our palace in Indraprastha, relaxing in the night breeze after intense lovemaking. He had lifted me in his arms and walked into his favourite block of the palace, the house of weapons. He placed me gently on the ground inside. The earth shivered, or maybe I did. I was led towards the collection, followed by brief introductions of which weapon was what and gifted by whom. I wasn't listening to him.

'You don't like it here?' he asked, amused.

Raising my wrist, Arjun made me touch them.

Some were frozen as if they'd been trapped under ice for ages; a few looked like pointed animal teeth; some curved like bird beaks at the edge; and some were so hot, they singed the fingers.

'No, I don't.' I pulled back my hand in disgust. 'These look like breathing beings with a pulse but no brain, empowered by cruel masters to kill.'

'So rude.' Arjun frowned in mock disappointment. 'Everyone is unsophisticated until they are trained or tamed.' He turned me towards him gently. 'These weapons are like leopards – solitary, elusive and unyielding. Their friendship is rare, certainly not for hostile abusers.' He winked. 'Most of the time, they are unpredictable.' His thumb pressed on my lips, coaxing them open.

'Why is Mother Kunti fond of Anga Raj?'

Dismayed with the sudden piece of information, his face hardened. 'Why should she be?'

'Why do you detest him?' I rephrased.

'I don't. I only retaliate in response.' He tried to remain calm, measured with his words.

'In response to what?' Sensing a bottomless pit below the surface I had scratched, I slid past him along the stocked-up layers of weaponry hoping he would follow. He did but did not keep pace. He walked with baby steps, talking more to the weapons hanging from the wall.

'He wanted to fight with me. I didn't.'

'Why?' I turned right and took a sharp left through the narrow pathway.

'Because I have nothing to prove. Royalty has given me recognition; it has also tormented me with baffling conflicts. People are not aware of the struggles. They look at the privileges. Naysayers claim that I title myself as the greatest warrior of Maha Bharat. I don't.'

I had asked two questions: Why Karn wanted to fight, and why Arjun didn't. Arjun chose to answer only the latter. Not a single word assassinating the character of his rival, none undermining his talents even for the pleasure of doing so. He walked unmindfully, following the jingle of my anklets.

'That day, the Pandav and the Kaurav brothers

were assembled for a martial exhibition. Karn appeared from nowhere and appealed to compete with me. They turned him away because I was a prince, he was not. They shouldn't have done that. Denying opportunities to deserving talent is an act of cowardice. I would have welcomed him if I could. There is a lot to learn from him.'

Was this really Arjun talking? Praising Karn standing inside the weaponry – his temple? Or was Krishna playing a prank again? I stopped at my spot, waiting to be found.

'You both are similar in many ways,' I provoked further.

This hurt. Appreciation is one thing, self-pride is another. Arjun didn't cherish the comparison.

'No, we are not. Mother Kunti is tolerant, not fond of him. Why are we discussing this?'

By now, I was tensed. I could hear Arjun, but couldn't see him. Had he stopped somewhere, too? The armoury had many twists and turns, the walls full of gigantic bows and scary arrows hanging on them. I had lost my way. I ran up and down the narrow trail only to find myself deeper in the chamber, the exit lost. I surveyed my surroundings desperately to figure out from where I had entered the building when gentle hands pulled me in and I was back in his arms. He walked me to the front. Faint rays of daylight fell on my face. The exit was straight ahead.

'Whose weapons are these? Yours or the family's?' I asked lethargically, my head on his shoulder.

'I owe everything to the family. Such is the rule of royalty.' He continued with a serious face, 'However, most of the weapons stored here cannot be passed down as inheritance or gift. They can't be stolen, borrowed or reused.'

'Who would you give them to if you could?' His fair fingers entwined with my dark ones, his other hand stroking my back as the ruggedly masculine smell of his body engulfed me in a trance.

'Bhishma, my grandfather. My first teacher of archery.' He paused. 'Or maybe, my mother. Not everyone can love her, at least not the way she wants to be loved.'

Bhishma! Kunti! I had been trying to bring Arjun to discuss someone else. 'You talk so generously about your mother. No love for your father? You fought with Devraj Indra to uproot the Khandav!'

Rebounding from his temporary melancholy, Arjun raised my chin towards his, 'You are remarkably casual about asking difficult questions.'

'I have heard that the Pandav were ridiculed for having two fathers—' I stopped abruptly. This was sensitive.

'The trick of dealing with tough situations lies in accepting them. We accepted the truth. It is a small tribute to our mother. My father is Pandu. Indra is my godfather,' Arjun ended the conversation.

I stared at the beautiful eyes, always passionately engaged with the present, which, for now, was me. I could feel the excitement pumping in his veins. Standing close to him, I could hear the thumping of his heart. They were the beats of my life too, the music of nature.

In response to this rhythm, the birds cooed, the brook splashed and the leaves murmured. Captured in his aura were the colours of spring and the harvests of autumn, punctuating the dry winters and balmy summers. Arjun's burning desire to savour life was Draupadi born to quench again and again.

*

How did I, the fire-born, receive and return such love for a son of the god who brought water?

'Opposites attract, Krishnaa.'

'But reverses can repel.'

'Not with you two. Forces in friction sometimes fall into an inseparable bond. Rules apply as much as they don't. Neither fire, nor water spares what comes in their way. They purify all. They burn or drown if besieged. No one is judged. You both are aligned by your values.'

*

'Khandav was home to the worst kind of wildness.'

What Khandav? Oh, I had asked Arjun about it sometime back. I snapped out of my reverie. Arjun and I were a few steps away from the exit of the house of weapons.

'Takshak, the corrupt king of the Nagas, built a military capacity comprising the *pisach*, the *rakshas*, the *daitya* and the *danav* by misusing his friendship with the devraj. Agni, disguised as a brahman, approached Krishna and me. He wanted his mammoth hunger to be met by setting the forest ablaze. That evening, my dharma clashed with Indra's and war was inevitable.' There was pride in his voice, having buried another episode in the pages of history, now reopening a closed chapter to pamper his melodramatic wife.

'I heard Agni gifted you the *Gandiv*, your celestial bow.' A mischievous look appeared on Arjun's face at my question.

'Not only the Gandiv, Agni has also gifted me the unthinkable arrow that will one day string to it.' He pulled out a gold pin from my braid, fixing it to his *uttariya.*[3] 'The arrow with a mind of its own. It will shoot not because I will it but only when it is prepared to. How far it will go, no one knows. What destruction will follow, only time can tell!'

I pulled myself away from his arms and turned around to face the walls. 'Which one?'

Arjun laughed. 'The one reluctant to be equalled with smaller weapons housed within closed chambers.'

A riddle again!

Frowning, I started walking out of the armoury. I could still hear him chuckling. I thought of locking him inside the colossal hall. But the punishment would fall upon me, he would treat it like a reward.

A few farmers and land diggers had got into a conflict, a concierge came to inform us. Yudhishthir had to settle a water dispute before attending to the land issue. Arjun had been requested to appear at the court. He proceeded in long steps.

---

[3] A kind of shawl.

7

After Takshak went absconding and his dependents were killed, one elderly man kept standing in the midst of the columns of flames rising upwards. Arjun lowered his bow when he begged for his life. In return, he proposed to rehabilitate the land. Mayasur introduced himself as the magical architect for boutique projects and refused to give us the architectural designs in advance. 'The spread of the house is determined by the personality of its inhabitants. I can only put together the stones.' He tried to be humble, irritating everyone with unsolicited philosophy. Mother Kunti commanded him to report to me.

I stood out in the open where the earth was being worshipped before the spade and bricks were brought in. Storm winds were propelling the holy pots in the air menacingly. A huge expanse of the dangerous land, once inhabited by the fierce and the poisonous, was turned to ashes overnight. Those living on it succumbed to fire, but not without spitting out all the venom inside them, which even Agni couldn't refine. The venom penetrated deep into the soil, as Khandav began its transformation into the breathtaking Indraprastha.

Nothing would last. Relationships would sour. All songs would fade into discord. Poisonous gases fizzled up from the earth, bubbles of terrifying curses formed over them and burst themselves.

'Indraprastha will be a kingdom of growth and prosperity, of beauty and integrity,' Maya prophesied with his eyes bored into deep sockets, pulling out a shrivelled creeper to tie his salt-and-pepper hair into an unruly pigtail. 'The universe will witness its lustre from afar. But it won't last long.'

'What does that mean?' I asked, unsettled by the proposition of a bleak future.

'The Takshak returns in the dead of night, when the rest of the world is asleep.' His hands were deftly negotiating a myriad instruments from his magical toolbox.

'To cause us harm?' I frowned.

Maya nodded. 'Takshak has lost his clan to the burning Khandav.' He adjusted the sacred thread around his neck. 'He slithers in to keep their ghosts alive. From destruction, the evil derives its strength. Takshak is plotting against the most powerful ones. Indra, for failing to keep his promise. Agni, for burning the forest. Krishna, for aiding Agni. Arjun, for plotting the destruction.'

'He can do nothing,' I declared.

'He knows that.' Maya placed the last piece of coal on the surface of a pillar and set it ablaze.

I stood up, perplexed. 'What are you doing?'

He didn't answer; an all-knowing smile flipped across his face. In the light of the burning coal, his eyes glowed like gold – the shine of an artist.

'From the large body of work I construct every

day, Takshak comes to destroy a little.' He closed his eyes as if he could envision the erstwhile Khandav chief, corrupting his masterpiece. 'The kingdom of Indraprastha will be as illusory as its namesake. I will finish my work much faster. The world will witness a lavish palace that can be designed only once in a hundred thousand years.' He spoke as if he was singing a song – a myth – neither completely true, nor completely false! 'What they will not see is Takshak's destruction. It will continue in silence, away from everyone's vigil, slowly but steadily. It will eventually shake the foundation, long after this generation has outlived its time.'

I stood up to take a walk. I was advised not to touch anything until I was given a thorough tour post completion. Maya stretched his arms, his eyes twinkling with creative explosion.

I drifted away. Some places in the construction site indeed seemed like ruins. There were grounds dumped with materials only Maya knew how to use. Sandalwood and soil of various colours, stale marigolds and fresh honey, tree barks and animal hides, rainwater stored in barrels, metals I had never heard of. He had asked for the coarse clothes and clay utensils we used during the time we spent in the Kamyak and Dvaita forests. He demanded for our bedcovers at Hastinapur and some chopped vegetables from my kitchen. Sometimes, he sat me down, asking me to relay the stories of the days left behind and the memories that mattered to me. I happily obliged. Why these were important, he never divulged. After a quick walk, I tiptoed back to Maya and found him levitating a few feet above the ground, crafting inordinate designs on the walls.

'The fire-born cannot wait to see things happen. She makes things happen,' he said, mixing philosophy with flattery. He poured water on the burning pillar and started cleaning the smelly, oily black soot left behind. I lifted an elbow to shield my eyes from the dazzling light. Maya's laughter flooded through the open frontiers. Slowly, I looked up. The pillar in front had sparkling diamonds all over its walls now. It trapped sufficient light during the day to keep glowing even after sundown. Mesmerizing. Terrific.

*

Over the next few months, I went back to Maya many times. I'd sit at a distance and witness the ruins transforming into an expanse of mystic brilliance. Sometimes he'd be polishing and painting the floor, making them shine like the Yamuna flowing inside a closed room. Some chambers served as the sauna, the walls plastered with aromatic clay and vapours emanating from above. I passed through them, getting drenched by the steam. Upon exit, I was soaked again by the torrential downpour in yet another chamber. Feeling ecstatic, I closed my eyes to welcome nature's jubilance. Arjun appeared from behind, his fingers running over my moist midriff, palms pressing upon my belly and pulling me towards himself. I could smell the passion of the wild. I turned to girdle my hands around his shoulders.

He was gone!

Shocked, I ran through the room to pull him out of hiding. But he was nowhere to be found. Disappointed, I walked out of the huge doors, which opened to a beautiful garden with beds of sunflowers and poppies and *rajnigandha*. Swift breeze adored them as they swayed to welcome a new visitor. My skin didn't feel wet any longer. I was enjoying a cheerful spring. Equally enchanted and confused, I rushed back to Maya. There he was, creating a bed of lotus on the pool. He laughed happily. 'There was no rain, Queen. Just the feeling of rain. Inside that chamber, all your wishes – in passing or eternal – stand granted. You feel what you desire is seeking you.'

I was filled with a strange anxiety. That night, I confronted Arjun.

'The inheritor of Bhishma's valour, the one who merits a partnership with Krishna, who is faster than Indra's horse and sharper than his *vajra*, yet fights the same deity for his Dharma. Can a person with a strong code of ethics be fair in love?' I accused him with forced allegations. 'If your devotion clashes with duty, which would you choose?'

Separating myself from Arjun's embrace, I lay down on the other end of the ornate swing, face down with my body half covered, suggestively available but purposefully distanced. The withdrawal wasn't meant to isolate. Arjun came over right away.

'Where is this coming from?' he demanded to know.

I sulked. 'Ram and Sita were pulled apart—'

'Let time prove it, Panchali. The keepers of Dharma have always qualified as loyal partners.' His fingers started tickling my bare back.

'Time!' I exclaimed, thoroughly disappointed. 'You have no promises to make?' The moon in its perfect round was privy to our conversation, bestowing its best charm to a sultry evening. An inculpating lover was nothing new to it.

Arjun slid his hand below my arm. 'Why do you trap me into the conventions of a clichéd lover?' Very softly, he turned me towards himself, sighing above my face and catching my breath with unusual warmth. 'My promises will engulf and overwhelm you in this lifetime of togetherness. I shall announce them if I have to. But I may reserve to myself the act of justifying my love with vows that shine like jewels but cannot meet the empirical obligations of the beloved.'

I narrowed my eyes at him, wondering if Indra's son could be this practical. He smiled.

'I am birthed by my mother too.'

*

Months whirled by. It was time for Maya to render a royal handover. I met him for the last time on that morning. The palace of Indraprastha sat on the erstwhile ruins of the Khandav like a gigantic crown, symbolic of opulence and hope. Its outer walls glittered with the reflection of the sun on the ripples of the Yamuna. An east-facing metallic pot planted on the roof pumped water from the river as a tribute towards ancestors. The water fell on the terrace pool with a huge swastika inscribed on the botttom and flowed down the palace pipes to be recycled.

Fantasy elements I wove while singing lullabies to the royal children were spread throughout the length and breadth of the palace. Motionless water was mistaken as a concrete passage between two chambers; the cool floor resembled a bed of burning coil; pleasant winds carried the fragrance of divine flowers; birds were chirpy and hymns from the wonderful Saraswati's mighty veena travelled unbarred through the nooks and corners of the mansion.

Elevators crafted by the oracle engineer took me to topmost floor. I looked down from there. The kingdom below spread its contours before my vision. Farmlands had sprung up towards the east. On the south, I could see the training centres for wrestling and swordfighting. Manufacturers of cotton and earthenware, artists and musicians, priests and professors settled towards the north. Collecting the commodities from there for distribution and sales, the traders had set up their offices in the west. Carts and horses ran through the well-built roads of the finely structured township, carrying people and their belongings towards growth and prosperity. Everything was systematised; everyone looked happy.

'When did the settlement begin here? Who are these people?' I chirruped happily, looking at the soulful mayhem below.

Maya laughed aloud. Inspiring is the happiness of an artist. 'Below is what I have taken the last fourteen months to construct, Queen. This is the reflection of the residents of all colours, castes and tribes across the country, benefitted by the Pandav brothers at various phases of their lives. The palace is only a reward, symbolic of the exuberance of the king and kindness of the queen. The greater the success of the leaders, the bigger will be the spread of the palace, loftier its roof.'

'And the pleasure inside the chambers?' I probed.

'Those are the queen's magical spirit of home-making transformed into divine elements used for the construction. A manifestation of Draupadi's journeys from the royal corridors to dark forests, turning difficult venues into a home with ease.' Maya inhaled the scent of the nascent creation between his fingers.

Astounded, I looked back at the robust life-force below. What more could we ask for?

'Unless the subjects are happy, a capital is only a Khandav,' Maya contemplated. 'For the world, I submit the palace of Indraprastha. This covert disclosure, I leave only for you.' He paused and looked around for one last time. I turned to face him. 'This palace is nothing but an illusion, queen, aptly named Indraprastha. It will mirror the status of the subjects ruled by the great Yudhishthir and Queen Draupadi.' Maya lowered his voice. 'Even if time ever forces Draupadi to abandon the palace, Indraprastha will never desert its queen. Wherever you go, the magic will follow. The edifice will one day be demolished by Takshak, but his destruction can only deconstruct the material bricks.'

He had more to say, or so I felt. But he withheld, bowed and left.

*

In a few days, the palace was to be royally inaugurated along with the coronation of Yudhishthir on the throne. The majestic Rajsuya yagna would be performed by the Pandav.

Indraprastha was no less than Indralok on earth. So said the relatives and friends who had started pouring in from the next morning. No one slept. The rooms allocated for the guests were generous with light. The cool air blowing from the Yamuna kept the weather pleasant. Freshly plucked fruits were placed in the centre of the guest rooms, where they were monitored and replenished at regular intervals by sincere stewards. The kitchen was stocked with rich dairy and vegetables vouching health and purity. The tempting flavours of spices and sweets left people salivating. The kings and the brave generals, the sages and the gandharvas preferred to take a tour of the palace, which we ourselves were only partially acquainted with. They laughed when the optical illusions threw them out of wit with fabricated imageries of fire and water, sand and storm. Enchanted and entertained by the natural luxuries, they blessed the Pandav and agreed that heroes of valour and integrity deserved to rule such a prosperous kingdom.

No one remembered Khandav; Maya was nowhere to be seen.

8

Father Dhrupad arrived late in the morning flanked by Dhrishtadyumn and Shikhandini. I stood behind Mother Kunti. She welcomed them by smearing vermilion and sandalwood on their foreheads. Shikhandini smiled; I winked back. A few hours later, I was glaring at Dronacharya as he waited to be received. For the Rajguru, the language of my eyes always remained as severe as it could. But this man had a thick skin. He avoided me, as much as I tried to embarrass him. My husband's teacher and my father's friend-turned-enemy understood the underlying disdain, conscious that my customary bows did not care for his blessings. Dronacharya and Kripacharya, a council member and teacher at Hastinapur, were led towards the east-facing rooms. For my father and siblings, I had reserved the chambers towards far west.

The first to arrive in the evening was the white chariot from Hastinapur. Protocols be doomed, I crossed the flight of stairs to stop right in front with umpteen glee. Sahadev opened the gate of the chariot. Granduncle Bhishma looked at me with immense affection and came forward to bless me even before he had greeted the brothers. He promised to see me in the evening, after he had attended the formalities waiting for him. Like a tiny bee circling its favourite flower, I nodded happily. Mother Kunti looked away.

She had never said a word against the grand old man, but I could sense her discontent. For some odd reason, she was cold and resentful towards him.

On a large silver plate, I placed an array of fruits and colourful sweets I had prepared. A blue velvet cover laced with golden thread was placed on top. As I passed the balcony, the colours of sunset waved over the Yamuna. The elevator took me downstairs where people were running their offices. Without knocking, I pushed the door open and barged into the conference hall. Bhishma was seated with the council, documenting the regulatory laws for the new country. Shocked by the invasion into their confidential summit, they looked for polite words to send me off. I stood at the door sternly, with no intention of retreating. Bhishma looked on for an explanation. When he didn't receive any, he burst into laughter and asked for the council to disperse. They got up slowly. The group looked confused at the unexpected indulgence of the senior general. Some were angry at the audacity of a younger queen. I stepped aside to make way for them. One by one they left, marvelling at the spell that diverted Bhishma from his unfaltering dedication to the country and the council – perhaps for the first time in his political career.

While I was enjoying the rare laughter of the grand old man, one attendee from the conference brushed past too close. A sudden icy cramp gripped my left arm. It was the breath of the Evil – anxious, jealous and insecure. I heard a profanity being uttered, pledging to smash the arrogance of the undeserving. I turned immediately to track its source. Reluctant well-wishers smiled leniently, showering blessings of generous growth and opulence.

I must have been mistaken!

The huge spread of illegible scripts on the floor decoded and reconstructed various social and political convolutions. Rolling out the blue velvet over them, I put down the silver plate and started slicing the fruits. Relaxed now, Bhishma allowed me to dominate his time with grandfatherly kindness.

'The tigress will never vacate her dominion, so what if the forestland is uprooted.'

I continued putting the sliced fruits neatly in a bowl, ignoring Bhishma's taunt. He pretended to be in distress. 'What will happen to the incomplete tasks if civilized gatherings are prone to tigress attacks?'

He looked down at the plate I was arranging

for him and then back at me. 'I have heard that man-eating tigress of Khandav can swallow the reputation of the king and kingmaker, both. Yudhishthir and I are endangered.'

This was enough. I pushed the plate towards him with great affection. He closed his eyes and breathed deeply in appreciation of the aromatic sweets.

'Perhaps the kingmaker should sometimes double up as a queenmaker,' I retorted.

The old man took a few moments to process each word and, once again, burst into laughter. 'Queenmaker! Does such a term exist?'

'Not until the attention of the veteran is forcibly revised,' I chuckled, leaving him in splits again.

He pulled the plate towards himself. Tired eyes revealed how badly he needed the break. In the banal world, the legends didn't have the luxury to express fatigue. They lived to break their own records till they died, leaving behind monumental legacies and faceless admirers. There was nothing in-between.

This was not the first time I had forced him to stop. This was not the first time he had resisted my interference and given in eventually. Back in Hastinapur, there wouldn't be anyone to water this huge, sheltering banyan. Hunger and rest are the obligations of the ordinary. Wasn't he Bhishma, the trouble-shooting extraordinaire?

The distinction between Hastinapur and Indraprastha felt cruel for more reasons than one.

I didn't realize when my eyes had flooded with tears. Bhishma noticed them. I turned away. He caught me by my hand and pulled me closer to him. We sat in silence, remembering the good old days. Endearing the grand old man had not been easy.

*

Preparations for the Rajsuya Yagna in Indraprastha were going on in full swing. Everyone had responsibilities allocated to them. The kings who performed this ritual won their eligibility to enter Devraj Indra's heaven, once their life in the earthly realm was complete.

I didn't see much of Arjun. For days, he wasn't even in the palace, attending to subjects in some corner of the country. On one of those evenings when I returned after finishing my chores, I found him snoring away with one leg hanging out of the bed, and the other sprawled across the rest of the mattress. Moonlight wrapped its shimmering arms around him. Haunting winds moaned like depressed Yakshis deprived of love.

'Some princes are pirates. They enter unannounced and exit on the sly,' I whispered in his ears grudgingly. He smiled in his sleep. I cuddled up next to him, placing my head on his chest. The heartbeats of the lover is a woman's lullaby. I passed off into deep sleep.

Early next morning, I sprang up to find him already bathed, wearing his armour and belt. I tried to get up hurriedly when he walked forward, pushed me back to the bed and planted an intense kiss on my lips. Pulling himself away with great effort, he readied himself for another busy day, his eyes lingering on me as I lay watching him lustfully.

Just when he trusted my lethargy, one of my legs went behind his knee and he slipped forward, face down. I covered his mouth with my palm. It was too late in the day for the palace to hear the jingles of love.

'I will be back, mischievous woman!' he rubbed his nose against mine.

Before stepping out, he stopped upon remembering something. 'Did something happen between you and Duryodhan in the last few days? Was there any terse exchange or argument?'

'No!' I sat up, frowning. And then I remembered. 'He was about to walk into one of the pools while critically observing the sculptures. I called out to alert him. He didn't look very happy about it. Mumbling something like '*I have eyes … I can see*', he moved on. Why?'

Arjun shook his head. 'Nothing.'

He left.

By noon, tongues were wagging. The rumour

spiralled around that I had called Duryodhan a blind father's son, who couldn't watch out for himself while walking. Duryodhan had vowed to teach me a lesson for my audacity. I shrugged.

This man, Duryodhan, was a house of strange complexes. Even if two birds brawled on the roof, he'd deduce their chirrups as a mockery targeted at his father who couldn't see or his mother who wouldn't see. Self-victimization is a shrewd art that can colour innocent remarks with hues of transgression. Muscular and large, with a fine range of elaborate jewellery inlaid with precious stones around his neck and arms, Duryodhan remained obsessed with his mace – oiling, rubbing and shining its surface, and practising combat moves with it. His trauma multiplied when the Pandav achieved something he didn't see coming.

'I'm proud of you, my son. Magnificence flourishes under your watchful eyes.' Dronacharya patted the shoulder of Yudhishthir, tersely looking at me from the corner of his eye. 'Keep growing, keep shining.'

Mirrors on the palace walls stooped ahead to angle themselves against the illumination of the earthen lamps, brightening the place further for the relatives to chat. Gazing at them angrily, Duryodhan interrupted the Rajguru.

'Don't be so dismissive of the blind king's palace. It bestowed shelter and honour on you when you didn't have any.' This jibe from the eldest Kaurav turned Drona red. But before matters turned ugly, Yudhishthir insisted that the sweets prepared by Draupadi be served to the esteemed guests. I obliged.

The eastern window broadened its boundaries, making way for the fragrance of blue lotuses in full bloom outside. The flavour of the snacks worked like appetizers. Plates were full, the attendants waited to serve more.

'Huh!' Duryodhan said after taking a huge bite. 'Too hard, cooked in haste. Even with her eyes covered, my mother makes better sweets. Draupadi must have tasted them but didn't heed the recipe.'

Bhim snatched the remaining pieces from his

plate and gobbled them down in one go. 'You are right. Panchali's sweets don't deserve your golden tongue.'

The crowned prince of Hastinapur sulked. He couldn't ask for more, neither would anyone offer him any. The others refilled their plates, hiding their laughter.

9

Yudhishthir's horse was ready for the Rajsuya yagna, after being bathed with milk and sandalwood water. Garlands piled around its neck. A gold crown adorned its head. Crimson silk embroidered with green thread was placed on its back. Mother Kunti smeared turmeric and kumkum on its forehead. I ran my fingers through the flowing mane and hugged its neck. It rubbed its mouth against my cheek. Amid auspicious chants of the palace priests, the horse galloped ahead with Yudhishthir. An army of followers went behind. The princes went out in turns, each assigned a direction and country to march towards. I joined my mother-in-law after seeing them off.

Often, while running various daily errands, I would steal looks at her. She had no significant expressions on her face, not even that of happiness. Every morning, without fail, she would serve water to the sun god and wait to watch the early morning sun assume its position in the eastern sky. I had always seen her follow the ritual – from behind the trees in the Dvaita forest after my wedding, and later from the opulent balcony of Hastinapur. The palace of Indraprastha misled the directions. The sun seemed to be rising from all sides; wherever one stood, the sun gleamed like it was the east. Kunti was the only one to never confuse the sun's real position. She looked straight into its radiance, whatever the time of the day, however intimidating its glare. At times, I felt she was talking to the sun, seeking answers, making accusations at the deity or simply discussing life!

This family and its mysteries never ceased to amaze me.

I tiptoed behind her and joined my hands before the sun. Her flickering lamp was held towards me, its warmth bestowing blessings.

'What is it, Draupadi?' she asked calmly.

There was gibberish scribbled on a slab of smooth rock kept before her. Lines and symbols lay drawn as usual, I couldn't decipher their meaning. Late in the nights and at leisure hours during the day, she would be writing, calculating, wiping the symbols all away and starting from scratch all over again. Sometimes she'd be happy with the results; otherwise, whoever was around would receive a piece of her mind. Insane are the pursuits of scholars, ambitious are the dreams of discovery. Their brains never retire.

'May I ask you something?' I tried to be careful.

'He conspired to find me company at a time when I wasn't looking for one. He never understood and I never explained. Does that answer enough?'

How did she know I was about to discuss Bhishma? I fiddled with the corner of my robe.

'This is your kingdom, Draupadi,' she added.

'You are the queen of Indraprastha. You are free to adorn the palace with elements of your choice. If the old general agrees, you don't need my permission to shift him to Indraprastha.'

Her words sounded like honey. I looked up with excitement and was disappointed immediately. Her eyes were shining, emanating confidence that Bhishma wouldn't ever leave Hastinapur. I stared at her, trying to gauge why such a ploy was at all necessary.

Much unlike Mother Kunti, I met people with exuberance, making friends easily. I played with the children of the house in the open meadows of Hastinapur. On returning, soaked in the monsoon rains, I was received by Arjun's broad arms. He pulled me into our private balcony, where peacocks danced and the mynah shouted expletives. Aunt Gandhari shrieked at the brashness of the royal bride and rushed to Mother Kunti.

'New brides should be disciplined on the very first day,' she advised, proudly pointing at the docile wives of her hundred sons.

Mother Kunti never said a word to me.

A few floors apart, Granduncle Bhishma was conducting a sword-fighting workshop. He trashed her concern. 'You have the throne and children and grandchildren, you have all the luxury and a royal title. Yet you have a problem with other people's pleasures?'

'A leader must be discreet. Women from royalty cannot run across the meadows, laugh aloud or romance openly!' she whined.

'Wrong,' Bhishma roared. 'A leader sets the discourse of a generation. Each leader decides their own path. Kunti did, when she moved out of the palace with Pandu. You did, when you pressed a cover around your eyes. Now let Draupadi take her own calls.' Granduncle Bhishma's tone was conclusive. 'If the children of the family are happier around her than with you, either be like her or let them be.'

Gandhari cringed at Bhishma's overt bias and tramped away angrily.

*

A messenger had returned with news. I rushed downstairs, putting an end to the irrelevant memories.

The Pandav brothers were being warmly welcomed by most of the lands. The transformation of Khandavprastha to Indraprastha was a fabulous success story, being discussed far and wide and adding to the Pandav glory. But success inspires those who are willing to learn; the rest feel threatened. Some kings stopped the princes, declining the invitation of friendship and declaring war. The brothers defeated the rulers and adopted their countries. The waves of exuberance honoured not only the Pandav but also the clan as a whole, carrying forward the legacy of the brave Bhishma. It was a rare occasion when the Kaurav and Pandav were united, jointly attending to allotted tasks. They laughed on the way, cracking jokes, reminding each other of myriad childhood foolishness and pranking each other all the while like cousins do. 'Such camaraderie would make one long for brotherhood,' the messenger gushed. Granduncle Bhishma rewarded him with gold coins.

Hardly did we know that, amid the unconstrained euphoria, the seeds of sin had begun sprouting. A big conspiracy was being hatched to transform the playful brothers into bitter enemies. The roots of the Evil only needed time and sufficient inattention to spread.

The magical palace of Indraprastha was filled with delightful conversations between men and women dreaming and discussing possessions and prosperity. No one felt tired, at any hour of the day people beamed with enthusiasm. The footfall of visitors increased. Travellers from far off countries and poets lost in a world of their own, observant artists and curious scientists availed our hospitality. Each person painted a different description of the palace upon return, their memories of the magic vastly different. Everyone had heard about the palace of Indraprastha; hardly any of them could specifically define the architecture and the adventures experienced on its premises. They returned charmed and enthralled with unique stories. Only one ascetic, old and delirious, his words somewhat rudderless, said before leaving, 'Watch out for the second floor.' It was unexpected, because after great food and stay, our visitors left with blessings and praises.

'He must be demented.' The attendants wanted to forget him and move on.

That evening I went up to the second floor to invite everyone downstairs as dinner was set out. This was the floor allocated to the family from Hastinapur. The corridor seemed wrecked by a heat storm, the paints on the walls and pillars of a newly built palace looking faded. Black smoke of hatred spiralled out from the corners, threatening to decompose the beautiful Indraprastha back to Khandavprastha. Shocked, I took brief steps ahead, hoping to discover an overlooked mishap or unreported wreckage. A sweet voice startled me from behind.

'How may I help you, beautiful queen of Indraprastha?'

I turned. Disguised as a dear relative with an affectionate smile pasted on his face, his roving eyes were attempting to grope my body. A wave of discomfort seized from me the strength of vocabulary. With a sudden, fast skew he bent to the left, brushing his shoulder against my arm as if the touch was accidental. I ran, my arm scalded by the contact and ears ravaged by the laughter of the Evil from behind.

It took me a while to get back my composure. I sent a cleaner upstairs to check on the second floor. She confirmed, everything there was spick and span – nothing out of place.

Was I hallucinating?

*

A thousand holy bells reverberated from the top. The night was as dark as *amavasya* could be. The colossal gates of an old, mysterious temple were locked. Somehow, I had still entered through them. The walls on the inside were fragile, but the iron doors were firm. There was no priest around. Vermilion marks attested that the temple was still in service. Huge trees swayed in fury, a heavy branch almost fell on my head. I was lost in the wild. How I had reached this dense forest,

I didn't know. I called out for the attendants at the top of my voice. My calls were drowned by fearsome grunts of the ghastly downpour. Knee-level water had reached my chest. The intensity of the rain was rising and nature showed no signs of mercy. Puzzled, I looked skywards. The wicked Takshak was taking its nocturnal rounds, passing from one tree to the other, bathing little birds and sleeping mice in its venom, celebrating the sadist display of corrupt power. I shivered.

Khandav! Arjun had burnt Khandav to ashes. Where was the gorgeous Indraprastha? How did I travel back in time? The water carrying the debris of the structures and floating remains of lost lives had almost reached my mouth. I choked and puked, before drowning into the endless depth.

I was dying.

When I gathered myself to chant the last prayers, the flute started playing. A long and resolute tune streamed out as if Krishna was right next to me. My eyes flung open. I was still sunk, Krishna was nowhere. The rays of the sun had penetrated the transparent water. From afar,

I could see Indraprastha. Khandav had vanished just the way it had appeared. From beneath the waters of the Yamuna, I heard the resounding bells of the royal temple, initiating the morning oblations. I tried to swim towards it, but couldn't. Takshak had entwined its tail around my leg. Pulling me from the other end, it made a spine-chilling disclosure: 'Indraprastha is the grandeur for a while; the Khandav will return to stay.'

I shrieked as loud as I could, with whatever strength I had left.

Strong hands held my body, moist with perspiration. I screamed more, writhing on the bed. Kind fingers patted my forehead. I could feel the warmth.

'What happened, Draupadi? Was it a nightmare?'

I sprang up on the bed. Mother Kunti was seated before me, watching with concern. I looked around. Everything was in order, in their right place, yet my heart thumped as if I had lost them all. I looked back at her. By now, she had lit an earthen lamp.

'Tell me about it,' she commanded.

I reached out to her hands, breathing heavily, and told her all I could at one go. She only sighed.

'How can I dream of drowning, Mother? What does this dream mean?' I asked nervously. 'Water is the tool of the Devraj. Do you think his son Arjun can cause me danger?'

'No, he wouldn't,' she said with conviction. With an equally cold voice, she added, 'But he might not always be there for you.'

'How can he not be there?' I asked. Anxiety refused to follow the decorum while talking to an elder. 'He is my husband; it is his duty to care.'

Mother Kunti didn't answer immediately. For some time, we both said nothing. I heard her eventually as I lay on her lap, trying to analyze in vain the prophecy behind the horrific nightmare.

'More important than who you are failed by is who stands by you. Krishna is with you everywhere, Draupadi, even in your worst dreams where Arjun can't reach,' she tried to console me.

My eyes filled with tears. 'I can conquer the world with one hand as long as Arjun holds the other. How can he detach from me – in reality or in dreams?'

Mother held my face between her palms. 'Arjun is after all a human, Draupadi. His attendance is inspiring but not devoid of limitations. Krishna is godly. Imbibe that power. The flute covers a radius, an arrow is unidirectional.'

10

The Rajsuya yagna had gone extremely well. Earthen lamps were lit in every house of the kingdom. Portions from the royal offerings made to the deity were distributed in silverware to every citizen. The concluding ceremony for such an overwhelming event left us relieved. We hit the bed, realizing for the first time how tired we all were. The palace doors closed, sealing every noise from the outside world. Porous roofs made way for the moonlight to percolate down the panels. Difficult ambitions remodelled into approachable dreams fondled the heavy eyelids of the relaxed occupants.

After a long time, Arjun was back at my side, without the liabilities of the day chasing him through the night. We both sank into deep sleep, locked within the folds of each other's arms, feeling protected, wanted and missed. The next morning, the Hastinapur family was to bid farewell. I clutched the granduncle's elbow, urging him to stay back. He blessed me with immense fondness, pretending not to notice the tears tingling in my eyes and looking away to hide his own. Duryodhan was extraordinarily pleasant during the farewell, sounding happy and generous in extending an invitation to the Pandav to join the Kaurav at Hastinapur and celebrate their prosperity over a friendly game of dice.

As much as they were settled in Indraprastha now, Hastinapur was home to the Pandav, replete with childhood memories. They lapped up the invitation. I saw the eyes of the Evil glistening. A crooked smile appeared on his face during the cordial family-bonding. I ignored that and immersed myself in the joys of the evening.

As they were about to ride their horses,

I distributed parting gifts to the relatives. Baskets filled with goodies included customized mementoes conveying love for the Kaurav. I had carefully designed one for Karn, too.

The Kaurav were accompanied by Karn for the Rajsuya yagna at Indraprastha, perhaps persuaded by Duryodhan into doing so. Throughout his stay, he had attended to his tasks sincerely, shouldered all responsibilities assigned to him, travelled with the brothers as one among them, even guiding and guarding them on weary nights while the others rested. Reserved, aloof but attentive, like a kind, older brother. Not a single anomaly in his countenance showed. He continued to look away, though, whenever I was around. With Arjun, he maintained a curt distance.

On this day, when I held out for him a basket covered with orange silk – his favourite colour – he looked up. Our eyes met. I suddenly felt my knees shaking. The basket dropped from my hands, its contents scattering on the ground. My head started spinning, and I almost fell on the stone portico. I would have fractured a bone or two if Karn had not been quick to grab my arm before I hit the floor. Others rushed in to help. Everybody agreed that the exhaustion might have taken a toll on my health. Apologizing profusely, I kept gasping for breath. This was my only opportunity to bury the hostilities from our past and encourage the continuance of a warm kinship initiated on the soil of Indraprastha. Karn's jaws tightened at the sight of the delicate endowment, now clumsily dispersed near our feet. I bent forward to pick them with care. I had placed in his basket the crystals he admired, seeds of the flowers he had loved in the garden, the books from our library he had turned the pages of, a gold bangle he had stared at on my hand as if it reminded him of someone. It took me days of minute observation to decode his tastes and acquire them from unbelievable sources. For the first time, he smiled as he watched the items I was hastily putting back into the basket. He bent down too, capturing the round fruits that tried to roll away or jewels that were hiding and handed them over. Gently, he released the basket from my diffident hand and bowed gracefully. I shivered again.

Standing so close to him, I couldn't help observe the anatomic similarities he shared with my mother-in-law. The large eyes, long ears, fair-skin turning pink at places, large forehead, thin lips and the dimpled chin – his features were remarkably similar to Kunti. There was a birth mark near his throat in light red that would go unnoticed by most. I had seen it many times in the cryptic symbols of Mother Kunti's studies. In Karn's arrogance and in his kindness, difficult and dutiful at the same time, I saw a lot that Mother Kunti had kept to herself. I was certain that Karn wasn't aware of this truth either.

I sighed, my heart going out to the Mother. I promised that this secret of Mother Kunti would be secure in my heart, till she chose to disclose it herself.

The Kaurav retinue left soon. I stood looking at it as long as I could. A few miles ahead, Karn turned around. Mirroring him at the same time, the Evil looked back too. Even after their chariots had galloped away, an inevitable truth stared at my face. The gratification on Karn's face wouldn't last long. The Evil would propagandize my fall as intentional callousness willed to insult the Anga Raj all over again. My efforts to call a truce would be wrecked. I closed my eyes, wishing I hadn't seen Mother Kunti in Karn. I wished I hadn't dropped the basket.

*

'Arjun is no ordinary being, neither are you. He won't be available to you in parts. Either he comes in his entirety, or he doesn't. That is his wedding vow to you, Draupadi. You are the only woman in the history of humans who will experience all aspects of your husband unpretentiously. Nothing will remain hidden.'

Mother Kunti had said this long ago, when I accused her of forcing five husbands on me. Her words hadn't made complete sense. It sounded equally appalling and enchanting. My husband being an open book for me was ideal and divine, but practically traumatic. If Arjun got infatuated with another woman, would I be privy to that too? Was I prepared for such honesty? I didn't think so. I wasn't asked either. Blessings were getting imposed one after the other, I couldn't deduce what to do with them.

It hit me hard when Subhadra entered Indraprastha. Subhadra, Krishna's sister and Arjun's wife. I was strangely drawn back into Arjun's house of weapons, this time alone.

'Krishnaa?'

I didn't answer.

'Krishnaa!'

No response again.

'My reflection weeps at your door; would you still keep it closed?'

I looked up this time, my eyes despondent.

'Your reflection. Arjun's apparitions. Can someone tell me why should I always receive love with such inadequacy? I was told that I have the whole of what the world will only receive in parts. No one explained that this whole is a glass showpiece, broken and scattered into five

disjoint fragments. Every piece is picked by someone else. I must still proclaim proudly that the non-existent whole is mine. Leave me alone, conspirator!'

All through the years of his exile, I heard about his weddings. The Manipuri warrior Chitrangada, the Naga princess Uloopi and finally Subhadra, the princess of Dwarka. Marriages that seemed more like treaties. Some political arrangements. But marriages, nevertheless. Why did he go on an exile? Oh yes, it was my folly. Playfully, I had picked his Gandiv and hidden it inside Yudhishthir's chambers. I had fantasized Arjun begging me to release it as I'd impose a queen-sized tariff for his obsession with the bow. In the meantime, news reached us that Takshak had stolen the cattle of a brahmin who had approached the third Pandav for help. Arjun burst inside the chambers and looked at me, crestfallen, before walking out in large steps with the Gandiv in his arms. Not a single word was uttered. He returned only after twelve years of exile with umpteen weapons gifted by powerful gods impressed by his penance, having signed pacts with reputed kings, three marriages gracing his resume and one of the brides towed behind.

Mother Kunti looked at me from the corner of her eye.

Arjun's armoury was never locked. The fading sunlight slapped upon the floor when I pushed the door open. This time the arrows and the swords in the house of weapons looked less boastful. They still shone from the walls, their polish blinding. Their length and sharp edges continued to threaten humanity. They had their own grouse against Arjun; I had mine. I felt an odd kinship with the weapons I hated. We all loved the same man. Did these arrows feel jealous when Arjun returned after each victory, proudly carrying a new weapon achieved by war or by blessing? I walked up and down the pathways in silence, wondering what the god-gifted armours were capable of protecting.

Could they protect a lover's heart?

'Is he in love with her?'

Startled, I smiled through the tears. Krishna had spoken for me again, raising the question that made me miserable, but I wouldn't have asked. The response came after a pregnant pause.

'Subhadra abducted Arjun.'

I laughed. The house of weapons laughed with me.

> *'Arjun didn't want to be abducted? She forced him?'*
>
> *'No, I forced him. Would you punish her?'*
>
> *'No. She is welcome. Why should I punish Subhadra for loving someone who loved her back?'*
>
> *'Would you penalize Arjun?'*

I stood before the Gandiv. Metallic, majestic, gigantic. And tempting. I had lifted and carried it so easily. The bow never objected.

'Each weapon is sensitive. They backfire when formalities are flouted,' Arjun had told me when we were here last time. 'If displaced by the unauthorized, this one exacts revenge by turning its owner into a slave, compelling him to obey or lose it forever.'

Then, I hadn't paid much attention. The words echoed into my ears now.

'No, I wouldn't penalize Arjun! Now leave, Krishna.'

I lay on the floor of the armoury in the company of Arjun's lovers. The man himself was with Subhadra. It was a sleepless night. The memories of unreserved romance in an open auditorium during my swayamvar left me pricked, bruised and scarred.

*

What a zestful morning that was! Panchal was pounding like the beats of a drum.

The flute played softly, whispering its notes like treasure of the wise and blessings from the elderly. Not everyone could hear the divine music. It offered me company when king after king failed to string the fish. Drishtadyumn was tensed about the failure of the event. The crowd had already started milling gossip, warning of misfortune when the swayamvar of princesses couldn't lead to a husband. In moments of distress, fiction sounds true. I had started preparing mentally for such a possibility. Suddenly the music of the flute started dancing into my ears with the notes jumping from one extreme to another, the tune shivering, flipping, oscillating with great pleasure. From the far end, a tall brahmin stood up and bowed with his hands joined. Next, he turned towards his right and looked at me!

This was awkward.

The man was staring with great charm, blatantly displaying his devotion in front of the public curiously watching. His eyes didn't wander upon my crown or the jewels on my neck, nor on the lavish garland I held. He gazed directly into my eyes, pushing the barriers, if any, with a besotted look on his face. Enticed, I marked his pupils responding to the rhythm of the flute. Here was the only other person in this crowded auditorium who could hear the music of my heart. Or was this the music of his heart too? I blushed. I would have got up and walked over to him, had Shikhandini not pulled me back.

He seemed relaxed, having already strung the fish into the eye!

The crowd didn't take too long to retort. They coughed and sneezed and murmured at a shameless brahmin's advances amid a brave gathering of mighty warriors.

'Did they know each other before?' someone whispered.

'Who is this brahmin?' someone else asked. 'He looks at her as if she is the only one present.'

'Lean, fair, well-built. Spectacular midriff. Bulging biceps. Now aiming for the princess. Such hapless brahmins claim to survive on aide.' The suspicion and sarcasm were both brazen.

'Has he never seen a woman before?' another person laughed.

'Why doesn't the father say anything?' This was an angry voice.

Various corners of the hall questioned the brahmin's character and Father's forbearance. I wasn't listening, though. Those moments were rare and thrilling, available for experiencing to a fortunate few. The brahmin was titillating me from a distance, ready to be judged, proposing the kind of love that survived the companionship of many lives. He promised neither riches nor fame. Our private exchange in the presence of a confused assembly swore that our union would make for a spectacular love story if so was destined. Feathery stubble, light grey eyes encircled in black, pointed nose, thin lips, crisscrossing veins on his forehead and curly hair sweeping messily around the shoulders. Fantasies were running wild.

Like a teasing friend, the flute made fun of his devotion and my appeasement, bringing us closer with its friendly jibes. The Brahmin bowed a little, seeking permission to proceed with the ritual.

What ritual?

I had almost forgotten that it was my swayamvar! Shy smiles flooded my face. I turned towards Father, who nodded in response. I looked back at the brahmin and returned the affirmation. Without wasting a word, he walked forward in bold steps, picked the heavy metallic bow as if it weighed no more than the garland in my hand, lifted the arrow, concentrated briefly on the water pot below and let the arrow take flight, not once looking upwards at the rotating target.

The tremendous clang must have been heard by the entire Panchal, if not also the neighbouring countries.

The fish dropped from the tall roof with a huge splash into the water below. Droplets from the pot sprang up towards the brahmin, moistening his chest and arms with congratulatory hail. He raised his face and folded his hands before my father who was shaking with overwhelming delight, ignoring the rest of the hall which had gone speechless. Shikhandini jumped out of her seat and picked the brahmin on her shoulder, honking and cheering in a way no one had seen her doing before.

People were so taken by the fall of the fish, they didn't notice that a loose yellow feather from the end of the arrow had come flying towards me, seated now over my jewelled bun. The soft quill tickled my shoulder. Where this did the brahmin learn such rich feats of romance? He had discarded the bow now and stood as if stringing such targets were a regular affair for him. He wasn't looking at me. He was receiving with humility the blessings of the other brahmins, who were overjoyed to witness such skill at archery. He was aware, though, that I was watching from behind, inspecting each part of his body.

This couldn't be the mere physique of a man, it was a poetry in motion.

My father hugged him. I was summoned to place my garland around his neck. My fingertips touched his back for a swift moment. But before I could fill myself with the pleasure of his garland falling upon me, he pushed me behind with force and turned in great speed, catching deftly a bow and quiver flung across at him. He positioned himself erect, pointing an arrow towards the south.

Shocked by the rude thrust, I had pulled up my defences, anticipating the brahmin to be an enemy in disguise. The doubt shattered soon. From the other end of the hall, a section of the kings had risen to revolt. There was a commotion amid raised voices, their teeth clenching in jealousy and anger.

'This swayamvar is nothing but a joke!' I heard a scream.

'Calling over the kings and handing over the princess to an ascetic? Such humiliation won't be tolerated,' there was another roar.

'Panchal will be destroyed. Today,' the gathering vowed in unison.

Shaken, I looked at my father. What I witnessed around was unbelievable. The brahmin before me had been joined by four others. Together, they formed a semicircle, keeping me in the middle. The other brahmins in attendance stood horrified in their section. Drishtadyumn and Shikhandini had joined the five brahmins, ready with their swords. Before anyone could fathom what was going on, an arrow flew from the bow right before me to make umpteen rounds over the heads of the revolting kshatriyas. A thick rope girdled around their necks and waists, tying them all up as prisoners of war, way before the battle had actually commenced.

How could I not be mesmerized?

No sooner had our corner erupted into a shout of victory watching the kshatriyas struggle at the other end, than another bouquet of arrows flew upwards and came right down, cutting the rope into a thousand pieces like a sword beheading the anarchy for its audacity. Bound and freed within a matter of moments, the kshatriyas moved apart in confusion, exposing the only valour who had dismissed the brahmin's attack with his own craft. He pointed his arrows at us now, as the others started taking refugee behind him. Confronting the brahmin was none other than the mighty Karn. Both men were targeting each other now, their bodies exuding tremendous power. The supporters on each side mindlessly ganged up to infuse bloodshed instead of passing fair advice. The other brahmins present in the hall threatened of dire curses, should the kshatriyas lay a scratch on a member of their community.

Men and their vanity!

Slowly, I moved out from behind the brahmin. Unhesitant footsteps made my presence felt as I positioned myself right between the two archers, open to be attacked from the front, all protective forces trailing behind. The gold on my body glittering in the rays of the sun cast bold reflections on Karn's *kavach*. The fingers holding tightly the string of his bow loosened. Distracted, his eyes fell on me. For the first time, he saw the woman he had come to marry, looking at him with utter disgust and accusing him of cowardice after having failed to win her heart and now leading a group to harass the one that did. The hands came down slowly and so did his eyes, looking at the ground in shame and dismay.

The crowd behind him nudged and pushed, questioning what had made the warrior retreat. Karn left the gathering with fast steps, without looking back once, with an unconvincing declaration that raising arms against a brahmin was against his faith. At the sudden withdrawal of their leader, the bravery of the rebels dismantled. Everyone turned towards me and so did the one who finally lifted the garland and placed it around my neck. Chants of the royal priest invited the blessings of gods, sandalwood and camphor invoked the aroma of union. Red vermilion was spread in the partition of my hair.

I bid farewell to the palace I grew up in. Father Dhrupad wiped his tears, Shikhandini hugged me and Drishtadyumn accompanied us with gifts from Panchal. The five brahmins took a diversion from the city, crossed the village meadows and entered the Dvaita forest. I learnt that I was in the company of the Pandav, who had been presumed dead by the rest of the world. The hands that spectacularly brought the fish down amid a crowd of failed warriors belonged to none other than the third Pandav. Their mother maintained a small and clean hut with amorphous equations scribbled with coloured stones on its walls.

With an eventful life changing at bottleneck speed, I placed the wedding garlands around every Pandav brother under the open sky beside the Kamyak lake.

*

Lying sleeplessly on the floor of Arjun's armoury while reminiscing the most beautiful memories of my life, I heard a tender voice calling me from outside, seeking permission to enter. Subhadra had arrived to seek my blessings. She had come alone.

11

Indraprastha prospered with each passing day, and so did its inhabitants. One morning, in the wake of spring, I was carrying a basket of freshly plucked marigolds and jasmines from the palace gardens, with lotuses in full bloom tucked carefully in between when I heard the excitement of my sons, making merry near the palace pool and practising stone throwing. The stones breezed past the ears and shoulders and heads of the attendants walking past. While the people cautioned, the children laughed and repeated their actions.

'Queen, should we start putting up the marigolds on the window frames?' someone asked.

Without thinking, I suddenly turned right. Sharp pebbles whizzed by in great speed, my head falling directly in their line of flight. The attendants warned, as did the children. Puzzled, I stopped in my path, forgetting to step aside. Just before the stones hit my forehead, a set of five pebbles rushed in from the left, colliding mid-air with the other stones and distracting them to the other side.

Saved from a grave injury, I uttered a prayer. An attendant ran to fetch a pot of water; another arrived with a fan. My children galloped forward, hugging, apologizing and promising to be careful. I touched their soft skin and flowing hair in consolation. Everything was fine.

I looked at my left.

Unruly hair. Broad forehead. It was difficult to turn away once he'd arrested someone in his magnetic eyes – big and deep like the ocean, a thousand waves lashing inside them. He sat quietly at a distance. A heap of fine, round pebbles lay beside him, the sling spinning between his little fingers. That godly smile on his lips was an imprint of Dwarka. Charming like his father. Indulgent like his mother. Reformist like his maternal uncle. A miser with spoken words, a liberal observer.

I walked towards him and handed over the basket of flowers. He fixed one lotus into his waist-belt, another he pushed inside my bun. Carrying the rest in his hands, his little feet darted off to offer help in lining the windows with marigolds. All through day, the lotus in my bun kept touching my shoulder gently, as if the petals were the tiny fingers of Subhadra's son, Abhimanyu.

*

Who am I? I sometimes asked myself.

When I was conceived, the astrologers had predicted I would be blessed with great fortune and my beauty would be discussed in kingdoms far and wide. That my eyes would be as large as lotus-petals, my complexion dark, locks curly. That I would resemble the aura of a nymph on earth, my body emitting the fragrance of a blue lotus, perceivable from a distance. The learned also predicted that the dark-complexioned girl would be remembered for bringing destruction upon many kshatriyas. The slender-waisted would accomplish the purpose of the gods.

Who knows the purpose of the gods!

The astrologers kept away one significant aspect of the truth. That the agent of change must go through an inordinate transformation herself.

I tried to see myself through the eyes of those around me. I was my father's pride as much as I was his sacrifice. For Arjun, I was a string holding his world together. For Shikhandini, I was the conduit for dragging her cause ahead without my knowledge. In the eyes of the Evil, I was an object of lust and envy. Krishna treated me like – himself! Bhishma handed over to me the custodianship of Devavrat; I was a window for the old man to seek escapades into the dreams and valour of his youth. Awestruck eyes followed me wherever I went. Sometimes they were laced with resentment.

'Why does she have a bluish complexion?'

'The wife of five men!'

'Born from fire?'

Confusions of the naysayers were many.

'The fire-born is as innocent as the fire. All consuming,' I heard Mother Kunti telling Aunt-in-law Gandhari. 'She will reduce to ashes all the veils that conceal the sins of the world. Her footsteps purify the path she treads.' I didn't quite understand her compliment. I still don't!

'Mother, did you love Devraj?'

This time Krishna didn't have to prompt. I asked her one evening, still disturbed by my deadly nightmare about Khandav. The feisty woman inched closer. I was afraid she'd hear the loud thumping of my heart.

'I do,' she said. 'I love Pandu, too.' She looked at me. 'Don't be so shocked, Draupadi. Love is not a ritual where rules cannot be amended. Pandu was the friend I never had before.' She waited, as if searching for an appropriate word. When she couldn't find one, she eschewed diplomacy. 'Pandu needed me. I needed him back equally. We were partners.' Mother's eyes filled with memories and melancholy. 'Our dependence on each other was an indisputable, metaphysical romance.'

I cried with her that night for Arjun's father, whom I had never met.

'With Indra, love was passionate. I brought Madri for Pandu, he united me with Indra.'

How beautiful and liberating was this acknowledgement! Simple, yet extraordinary. I sat soaked in the divinity. Mother Kunti was transported to another era, as she spoke about the Devraj. 'Indra didn't come as a mere individual but as an entity, exactly how I wanted. He came as a king, partnered with his best generals. Dharma, Vayu, Ashwini Kumar. Even before I blinked, Indra had spread his fabled *indrajal*. One mortal stood in between, his shadows were cast in the four directions. The world witnessed the birth of five sons one after the other, three mine and two from surrogacy.'

Mother Kunti indeed had poured herself fearlessly to the fire-born, with complete faith in my capacities to absorb. She looked beautiful and rebellious, encouraging a friendship without crossing certain boundaries. I was clutching one of her hands by now. She held mine back. 'The world knows the Pandav for their valour and brilliance in intelligence and warfare. The only weapon to crush the Pandav is to divide them, nothing else can destroy the five.' She raised her hands and blessed, her eyes restlessly moving over my face and appreciating the contours of the dark skin. 'You are the chosen one to keep them together, Draupadi. Such a feat cannot be accomplished by the ordinary. Getting you married to my sons wasn't a slip of the tongue. It was deliberate. Else I would have to convince all and that would be embarrassing.'

*

'Krishna, of the five faces, who do you think loves me the most?'
'Whomever you love the most appears to be loving you the most, Krishnaa.'

'Why do you know everything? Sometimes, you should just listen and share an opinion after careful deliberation. Can't you ever pretend to be less godly?'

Krishna didn't answer. The flute spurted notes in its own mystical language, wandering around and afar.

'Out of the five, who do you think can cause me pain?'

'Yudhishthir.'

'Yudhishthir? The epitome of Dharma? How is he capable of harming me?'

'Idealists are difficult to navigate.'

*

A few days after, we entered the palace of Hastinapur amid welcoming chants. Every face had a smile. Queen Gandhari greeted us at the entrance and escorted us inside with great affection. 'Feel at home. Though this grand mansion, I fear, could be too old-fashioned compared to the modern luxuries you are used to now.' She took out her gold chain and placed it around my neck.

'Wherever we might settle, in the opulence of a palace or the wilderness of forests, Hastinapur remains our home,' Mother Kunti replied, her tone caring but distant.

The cousins slapped each other's backs, pulled each other's legs and broke into laughter, bursting with youthful energy. The usually reserved Yudhishthir mimicked Duryodhan's childhood whining to his father, demanding everything that wasn't his. The eldest Kaurav's face went dark. He quickly recovered and retaliated with tales of a lazy Bhim getting scolded by Guru Kripacharya for floating like a tadpole in the river while the others swam ahead of him. The wives and sisters laughed. They flaunted the rising list of achievements of their children and sweeping victories of their husbands, all having resulted from their strict vigil on lifestyle and livelihood.

Was it only me who smelled something burning?

Not the holy fire that purifies but devastating

fire that wreaks destruction. It was the smell of burning flesh from the cremation grounds. Everything seemed perfect. The food was delicious. Nothing was out of place. Yet I was sceptical. The children took me to the garden – this time as a guest at their house – to show me where the swan had laid its eggs. Amid sharing recipes with the women and counselling on the maintenance of a personal treasury, I heard of a massive dice game being planned for the next morning.

'Why does the eldest Pandav fall for this dice game? He will again lose the hand miserably ...' The sarcasm of Duryodhan's loyal servant was cut short by another, nursing a broken heart since the Pandav had left Hastinapur.

'You won't understand this, brother,' he said. 'King Yudhishthir does it on purpose, making himself the object of laughter for his smug cousins. The Kaurav brothers can score over the Pandav only through treachery. Dice is a game of cheats, Dharmaraj will invariably fail.'

The first one groaned. 'Losers have many explanations, a thousand excuses.'

'Fools never understood King Yudhishthir's

game,' the other one smirked. 'Duryodhan and his maternal uncle, Shakuni, bask in the glory of winning a sport that the eldest Pandav had never played.'

I moved on. It was not for me to eavesdrop on arguments between servants.

That night, I started menstruating. It was untimely. If the discomfort of the anxiety wasn't enough, intense cramps started rising up my stomach. When everyone was enjoying the festive jubilance, I shrank into a corner. I chose to stay indoors over venturing out in stained garments. A few floors below my balcony, they all lay on the grass – eating, drinking, merrymaking. I couldn't hear them clearly. Nakul said something and got slapped hard on his back by a cousin. The fourth Pandav emptied the liquid from his glass on the cousin and fled. Others chased him, and once they caught him, everyone fell upon each other, laughing.

Could all these be an ordinary sequence of events?

Observing them from a distance, I sensed the

bizarreness of the situation. The Pandav weren't behaving like the Pandav. The Kaurav weren't behaving like the Kaurav. Nothing was artificial, yet something was unreal. What was this evening indicating?

Usually by this time, I would hear the holy chants of Mother Kunti. That too was absent. Only an eerie silence shrouded around, passing a hint of caution but failing to communicate with adequate clarity. Something was brewing somewhere. Else, why was Krishna missing? I wanted to see Arjun badly, but it would be silly to pluck him off the excited reunion ensuing downstairs. I closed my eyes. The flute raised its pitch, overwhelming the world with its resounding musical notes.

'Krishna, why aren't you here?'

'I am following you everywhere, Krishnaa.'

'Why has my talkative friend been silent for so long?'

'I am your intuition, Krishnaa. The inner soul. You were telling me how suffocating this stay is and how contrived the invitation feels.'

'I never said that.'

'You may not have. But you did.'

'Krishna, why do I sense danger? What is this burning smell all around?'

'You are right, Krishnaa. The passing hours are signalling a phase of transformation, when brothers won't be brothers, relatives will become strangers. Where dear or distant wouldn't matter. Expect a war, Krishnaa. A devastating one, a demanding one and a levelling one. One that questions morality and rationality, where duty remains as the only constant, the rest burns on the pyres. That is the burning smell you perceive. Fire purges everything.'

'But why now? Is someone dying, Krishna?'

'Yes, Krishnaa. You!'

Krishna never minced his words. I shouldn't have asked that. I sat up, distressed. Would I be assassinated, or would it be a peaceful death? Would the culprit be an enemy of the family? A rebel from the state? Or a deceitful palace guard? A scout from a hostile neighbour? But why! I remembered the dagger gifted by Mother Kunti long back in the Dvaita forest, during those lessons of martial arts. It was lying unused somewhere. I hardly ever carried it with myself.

'Not every death takes from you your right to breathe. Sometimes death occurs by stripping away the old faith that was once absolute, obsolete now. This is your battle, fight well.'

'Krishna! Tell me more. I must know what I am getting into.'

'I can't, Krishnaa. I am only as powerful as your intuition. I can't read the future.'

'What should I do then?'

'When death comes, embrace it. Feel no threat, have no fear. Shed the defunct, emerge afresh. It could be painful. Transformation always is.'

12

I clutched the sheets on my bed. Why couldn't Arjun see what I did? Why do women get premonitions that a man wouldn't? An abysmal night crouched outside. The leaves puffed out rowdy air, flowers drooped on the sides and vultures took tireless rounds looking for flesh. The sky was clear, but the moon was eclipsed. It was visibly not one of those days when Arjun was in control. Godfather Indra was asleep. I felt depressed.

The following morning, the cheer and excitement from the royal court reached all parts of the palace. The dice game had begun. The brothers were having fun with their cousins. With every hand at play, the cheers got louder. I didn't care for what Yudhishthir was losing again. So strange was his perseverance that insisted honesty must win even at a game of deception.

Just when I was preparing to take a bath, there was a loud knock on my door. I looked behind and adjusted my clothes. The guards had been instructed not to allow visitors. The knock sounded rude and intrusive, not how anyone sought permission to enter the queen's chambers. My hands and feet slackened. Was it time? I crossed my arms to clutch myself, pressing upon my elbows on either side with the fingers. I prayed and pledged. Whatever be the level of torment, I wouldn't be intimidated. The knock repeated, this time louder than before. I unlatched the bolt to a red-eyed attendant I had seen hanging around Duryodhan and his brother, Dushasan.

I had been called to the court of justice!

'For what?' I demanded.

'Yudhishthir has lost everything in the game of dice. His kingdom, his brothers and also his wife. The royal prince has sent for you.' He was looking me in the eye and circumvented calling Yudhishthir a king or addressing me as the queen. The palace attendants usually looked down while approaching the royal family. He must have been instructed to treat me as an equal.

So this was it. My killer was inside the family. For a moment, I couldn't decide what felt more offensive. The audacity of Yudhishthir or of those who had sent the attendant to my door. My body shook with rage. 'I don't belong to anyone to the extent that I can be given away. Go, tell your masters. The malversation of the Kaurav will elicit suitable punishment.' I spoke calmly but my voice, clanking like edged swords, reached all corners of the palace by some mysterious mechanism. It shook the walls of Hastinapur where crimes of many generations were annexed as indomitable gallantry, sinful karma justified as a minor compromise to fulfil exceptional obligations. Bhishma stood up from his seat, as did Vidur. Stunned, Duryodhan panicked. Even I was shocked. My voice wasn't quite mine. Some other woman dormant inside me had suddenly woken up. I heard the anxious voice of the Evil, calling upon all his henchmen to unite. He vowed to silence the woman who had dared to sound braver than men.

Soon, there were footsteps outside my door. This time there was no customary knock. The door was kicked open, its latch banging against the wall in protest. Standing in the middle of the chamber was the Kaurav prince, Dushasan, prepared to unleash his fury on an unarmed woman. The younger brother of Duryodhan, who had once warmly received me as his sister-in-law, now charged forward, making lewd remarks. His eyes were vulgar, hovering over my body. Clumsily, he clutched the back of my head and tried to pull me towards himself. I slapped him hard on the face. His escorts stepped behind, horrified.

The man flaunted his masculinity by dragging a woman by her hair through the open corridor, hauling the chaste like an accused, shouting perverted profanities about her upbringing and femininity. The long, wavy hair, which Mother

Kunti would oil and pull together into a perfect bun toiled like an iron chain in the hands of the corrupt. The attendants, men and women marvelling at the might and justice of the dynasty stood aside, watching the unfortunate fate of the queen who had just been impeached. They did nothing to block the lawless path of the deviant.

My attire was wet with menstrual blood. Drops of red stained the floor, which I had been hauled across. Inhuman force pulled me to immodest, merciless display of womanhood, in cruel violation of privacy. I crumpled under that touch, feeling small and spent. I squirmed to set myself free from the monstrous grasp. I felt dirty. I felt guilty, for reasons I could not explain. I felt responsible for everything that was happening to me. With both my hands, I tried to thrash the predator. His grip only grew tighter, hurting more. My anguish was the sinner's entertainment. Under such invasion, I experienced the helplessness of a woman – hopelessly compromised before the wicked, wriggling to hide herself, ashamed of nature's bountiful giving to her, constrained to believe that her biggest strength was her worst weakness. Even if I discarded the body, would the soul ever forget this encroachment?

Dushasan brought me to the open court and pushed me to the ground. My head struck the hard surface, oozing blood.

There they were, my husbands, bereft of their strengths, held captive by their cousins. Granduncle Bhishma was sitting in his corner, his eyes bursting out from the sockets, but mouth numb. The edges of his golden seat were smashed into dust under his helpless fingers. The most qualified servant of the king bound by an immortal vow was not authorized to rise against the throne.

I didn't look elsewhere, no one else mattered.

Transformative indeed it was, to breathe in a lawless court where brothers were estranged, relatives were enemies, the living didn't know they were long dead. How would the deceased rise against disgrace?

The laughter of the Evil reverberated through the open court. I looked at him for the first time, right into the eyes I had so far been avoiding. Shakuni. The king of Gandhar, brother of Gandhari, maternal uncle of Duryodhan. A short, fair man with thin, green eyes, smiling to expose sparkling teeth below a thick moustache. Beaming with delight, he suggestively shed his purple shawl embroidered in gold, crudely uncovering a repulsive body throbbing with libido. For years, had the Evil been nurtured under the negligent eyes of the indulgent family. His deceitful fangs bred in secrecy, overpowering the minds of the weak and influencing their actions, taking his protégés so far away from nobility that they had lost their path of return. Today, he had multiplied into a gigantic serpent with a thousand heads and a long tail, suffocating Bhishma and rendering the Pandav brain-dead with his venom.

Seated on his right was the rebellious Dronacharya, shaken into silence by the royal seat that equalled him with my father. He had claimed half a share of everything that belonged to King Dhrupad. Didn't that bestow upon him an honorary fatherhood towards me? Just as Father had predicted, when circumstances demanded him to lead from front, he eclipsed behind safe reticence. Also silent was the honourable minister Vidur and the dynamic teacher Kripacharya. With his overpowering venom, the serpent drowned the protests of Vikarn, the only pragmatic son of the reigning monarch. I saw the clones of the terrifying reptile in the heinous tolerance of Dhritarashtra, in the spiteful Duryodhan, in the malicious Dushasan and, to my extreme shock, in the vengeance of Karn. Anga Raj supported Shakuni, saying, 'A woman married to five men is no less than a prostitute.'

'Come, beautiful maid. Sit on my lap. Let me closely devour the beauty you are so proud of.' Duryodhan made an obscene gesture. Shakuni and Dushasan laughed, as did the other brothers. No one paid attention to Vikarn's laments.

'Dushasan,' Duryodhan called out. 'Why don't you strip her out of her modesty? For once, may her arrogance fall to the ground and get trampled under our feet.' Dushasan hurled abuses at me, refusing to touch my clothes and mocking at the blood stains on them. He cracked sordid jokes, uttering the choicest of words and made presumptuous digs at my nights with five husbands. He went on to describe my body parts, pleasuring the open court with the perceived nudity of Draupadi, treating a queen like a courtesan.

In the country of the blind king, everyone was blindfolded. Everyone was deliriously content in overlooking the obvious. I was no less guilty than the rest; else, why had I ignored the salient indicators earlier? The collective laughter of the Kaurav and the filth of Dushasan rushed in like a cluster of pointed arrows. I clashed against them all by myself. Amid tremendous sacrilege in the midst of a populated courtroom, the naïve princes of Hastinapur brazenly betrayed the trust of its people. The hall of justice set a severe benchmark of horrendous criminality. The Pandav lay drugged in a corner, motionless and powerless under the influence of some inexplicable spell. All our competence, all virtues that brought us fame, all privileges we were bestowed with were rendered useless when they were needed the most.

In the face of crisis, people fear of unforeseen losses. When there is nothing left to lose, the anxiety falls apart. Some kind of unexplained power raises its head. I seemed to understand why Krishna said I would die. On the verge of death, there is nothing to own. Not even the body, neither an identity. I closed my eyes, calling upon Krishna.

> *They want to see you pained and insulted, Krishnaa. Refuse them the pleasure. Defeat them by tiring them. Stay untouched by the dirty hands. Don't feel repentant for a crime that is not yours ...*

My body relaxed, slowly. The spine straightened again. Hands dropped on the sides, the knees were back to full strength – releasing from the ordeal that kept me coiling inside. Their words still affected me, but they ceased to hurt. I had sufficiently disassociated by now from the person called Draupadi. Like a flicker from the abyss of fire, I waited for the princes to perform every savagery that they were yet to explore. The Kaurav desperately tried to scare and shame, dipping to new lows with every new advance. They called Draupadi's husbands a bunch of lowly haggards who brought disrepute to the royal dynasty. Draupadi's children were dubbed bastards. Draupadi's complexion was ridiculed for being as black as the bottomless underworld. Draupadi, they agreed, was a buxom wench notoriously available to five men, setting immoral standards for the women of Maha Bharat.

13

Breasts. Limbs. Spine. Arms. Naval. Genitals. Pelvis. Not only did my body parts feature in Dushasan's lewd fantasy, but he also included crass comparisons with other women in the palace and beyond. The wives and attendants, musicians and poets, diplomats and streetworkers, brahmins and tribes – he equalled all women on his passion platter, spitting out raw hypothesis on how my fingers would pleasure a man and how my legs would part in similarity or contrast.

'Walk before me, lovely lady.' Dushasan's eyes stripped far more than his hands could. 'One look at your posterior and I can tell which side of the bed you'll turn to moan.'

Pathetic giggles arose amid the gathering.

'Dare you jokers underestimate the skill,' he trumpeted. 'It didn't take me many nights of practice to deftly peel the covers off virgins and wantons. They happily spread their buttery chests, be it on urban silk or forest grass. It's about time that I told you more.'

'Feel the shame, ancestors and leaders of a great dynasty!' Vikarn cut him off midway. 'A glorious past is rebuking the gruesome future as the bravest leaders of the country revel in a historic embarrassment. If no one else will, I will stand before Draupadi to fight for the honour of the dynasty and the country.' But before Vikarn could proceed, his brothers trapped him from behind, took him hostage and abused their youngest sibling for spoiling their sport. I stared as he fought against them – a lonely soldier rising against a bunch of tyrants. He kept trying to free himself from the hold of his brothers.

'This dynasty is the tale of many fallen heroes, Vikarn. They hide behind gigantic armours. Draupadi will remember forever the dauntless man of this era, who retains the rectitude to protest against impropriety,' I declared, without removing my eyes from the struggling warrior, startling the dispersed princes. The voice once again amplified on its own, echoing in every corner of the historic palace, unwilling to stay insignificant in the succession of secret sins. My face crumpled in aversion towards the Kaurav. I called upon Krishna once again in my heart, praying for his power to be mine and my vulnerability, his. 'Wait for the destruction, cowards.' I looked at Dushasan. 'My hair that you have touched will henceforth remain open. It will be braided only after I wash it with your blood.'

Distressed, Vidur rose from his seat to speak to the king. His voice dissolved in the roars of Shakuni.

'A lowly maid dares to curse the king's men! Is this what you were waiting for, Duryodhan?' Leering at me, Shakuni challenged his nephew, 'Rise and shine. When will you behave like a man? Or are you scared of this vile woman?'

The provocation worked. Duryodhan sprang

up from his seat. 'Patience, Uncle Shakuni. Why are you so keen for a wretched body sucked already by five drunkards?'

Laughter soared again.

Vikarn tried to get up, only to be pushed back down. Vidur collapsed. Bhishma, still looking down, removed the garland of pearls gifted by the gods for his vow and threw it on the ground. An emerging dust storm pulled apart its strings. The pearls travelled wherever they could, disappearing inside the earth, all accolades scattering like poisoned fruits.

'Are you here to watch and speak or action will follow?' Duryodhan pushed his brother and sat in front waiting for an opera to begin.

*

'Krishna!'

'Following you everywhere, my friend.'

'Give me strength ...'

'You own an ocean, Krishnaa. Discard everything you ever nurtured in your heart for the sinners.

Let go of all love for those you regarded as family. Trash every blissful memory that can inspire forgiveness. Whatever you drop will get woven into an inexhaustible fabric and wrapped around you. The foolish won't realize what he is pulling apart. Until you have something to discard, you will never be bare.'

*

Dushasan hurled forward. Whatever came in contact with his fingers he pulled with a war cry, laughing like a maniac, his desperate arousal cheered on by the gluttonous eyes.

Out went the cover of kindness and love, the sensitivity and warmth, devotion and fondness, humility and compassion, empathy and affection. God knows what else. Indeed there was an ocean to disown, trapped inside the attachment binding a woman's heart into a mesh of magnanimity. Infinite integrity gathered into a web of fine threads sliding like silk through the hands in haste. Memories of playing with the Kaurav children in the Hastinapur garden wove into the morbid interlock. With memories went away the trust of a human unto human. Also dissipating was the intimacy a jovial heart might feel for its kin. Increasingly, I started feeling lighter, the heart less heavy. Dushasan kept pulling with gusto. A flood of matter entwined into the delicate yarn, everything pleasant was disowned. They piled on the dirty floor where the Evil had laid his greedy footsteps.

Fallen from its grace was the honour of the courtroom. With every pull of Dushasan, the pretence of the Kaurav was undressed. Stripped off their chivalry, they stood naked amid the hall of fame, their conspiracies severely revealed and their cruelty condemned by mortals and immortals alike.

'Whore.'

Dushasan shouted in frustration and panted as the never-ending drape continued to grow. No amount of unrobing could denude the chaste. It only put the men to shame, for having molested the court of justice with their brazen obscenity.

Virtues of the feminine mountained beside him in endless folds. I was far from bare.

Some brothers still laughed at me, a few uttered profanities. Others had gone silent. The revered stars of a galaxy, once radiating with eminent talents, were derailed from their orbits, casting aside all morality that fastened a constellation together. With each pull at my attire, Dushasan shadowed every glory of the Kaurav. The infamy would stick to him forever as his only identity.

On this day, I was not the only one that changed for life. Krishna changed too. I never heard the flute again. It was replaced by the call of the conch shell, playing long, loud and shrill, invoking a war cry inside me, depriving me of sleep and peace as long as the Kaurav breathed. No joy, no happiness remained the same.

Dushasan fell to the ground, breathing heavily with exhaustion. The erotic vocabulary had disappeared. His hands were blistered; I was unscathed. Behind him, Duryodhan continued cheering. Shakuni reprimanded him for boasting about his trysts with the nymphs when he couldn't even effectively scandalize one woman.

The ugly, tasteless jibes were steady, though subdued, when a sudden hush fell over the hall. Warm hands touched my shoulder from behind. Without a word, Mother Kunti came forward to stand before me, challenging the royal court like a raging lioness. Distaste poured from her eyes. She stared at none other but Karn, as if his striking had mattered the most.

'This day will have consequences, my dear boys.' The words fell like irregular lumps of ice between a sudden hailstorm. 'The fluid that flows down her legs to stain the ground has set a wheel in motion. The earth has tasted blood. Till one man from this clan breathes, its thirst won't be quenched.'

Pulling me after her out of the royal court, Kunti held my hand firmly within hers. No one stopped her. With her unexpected arrival, there was a sudden shift in dynamics. The court was coming out of the spell cast by the Evil. Amid the commotion, Bhishma lamented, 'Does anyone remotely understand the curses she just pronounced? Did anyone hear Draupadi's prophecy? Everything we have built over generations through ambition and sacrifice is now on the wane. All I can do is to stand and perish. I will do so, because in Draupadi's resentment dies the pride of this clan.' He crashed on the floor below his seat.

A frightened Dhritarashtra tried to intervene.

'I regret what happened, but don't worry, Uncle Bhishma. I will send Gandhari to console Draupadi. Things like this happen in every big family. Masculinity seeks obedience from women. Draupadi has always been incapable of it.'

He received no response from his loyal officeholders. The silence that witnessed the humiliation of the Hastinapur throne continued to extend its favour. King Dhritarashtra modified his stance. 'My sons are innocent; they don't realize the repercussions of their actions. Let us bury the past and move on for the sake of the state. Aren't kings supposed to focus on issues bigger than a game of dice? Are we to stay confined in the politics of women? Kunti and Draupadi will have to understand.'

He would have gone further, entwining words around a fallen Bhishma, had Vidur not stopped him.

'This time the escape won't be as easy, King. We have seen all that you chose not to. The uprising of the Pandav will cost you far more than a kingdom.'

Dhritarashtra vehemently chided Vidur for his outburst, problematizing the issue beyond deserving attention and instigating the subordinates.

As we walked towards my chambers, the attendants stood motionless. The palace of Hastinapur was quaking with a sonorous voice pledging to break the thigh of Duryodhan where he had invited me to sit. It also promised to tear apart the chest of Dushasan and colour Panchali's dishevelled hair with his blood. Bhim had awakened from the intoxicated stupor. Hearts trembled. Mother Kunti didn't enter my chamber. She ushered me in and shut the door from outside.

*

This was the same room from which I had been forced out in the morning, the same corners I had wanted to latch on to, the dangling mirror I avoided during my menstrual days. I stood before it now.

Every morning on a usual day, I smeared sandalwood paste on my body and fragrant oil in my hair after bath. I coloured the partition of my hair with vermilion, coiffed the hair into a bun – often lined with the soft flowers Arjun brought home. My neck and ears would be adorned with queenly jewellery. I attended the royal treasury checking on the accounts and the assets, aiming for appropriate resource allocation that would bless the households with affluence and prosperity, fulfilling the need of every individual in the estate. The mirror reflected a woman in turmoil today, as dark as the amavasya, the palm of her hand stained in blood, hair unkempt, her tongue sticking out with insatiable hunger for human sacrifices, impatient to suck the life-juice out of a degenerated race. The people I tried to love and care for – in spite of their shortcomings and deformities – I saw their skulls garlanding around my neck, threaded by the mortal remains of Takshak. The beautiful chamber looked like a burial ground, with the ashes and smoke of the dead emitting a pungent smell. The red eyes overflowed with roaring anger. I felt connected to this other woman in the mirror.

The shining glass showed me innumerable faces from before the time I had been born – faces that had endured cruelty and let it pass or had been taught to accept it as fate. A huge population living in the Maha Bharat had been blunted, their stories censored and shoved aside. Among the images of countless women on the glass surface, I saw Amba, now reborn as my sister, Shikhandini.

*

There were voices outside my door. Queen Gandhari had come to meet; Mother Kunti sent her away. The elderly lady pleaded, accusing her brother and her sons of lost wit. 'The king has liberated the Pandav. Their lost wealth will also be restored.' She tried to reconcile. 'What more should Draupadi want? Tell me, sister, I will get everything for her.' She wept.

Kunti didn't budge. One by one, she sent away Bhishma and Vidur and everyone else. My husbands too were stopped on their way; they left promises and apologies at the threshold. Like a royal guard, Mother Kunti stood by my door all night. Her unwavering attendance in immaculate white clothes sent ripples of fear, muffling the well-rehearsed speeches of every monarch that came to offer consolatory advice to their favourite daughter-in-law.

14

Early next morning, when the birds chirped in the darkness, I looked again at the door. The shadow of Mother Kunti remained static amid the flickering lights of the torches. She hadn't slept all night.

I opened the door to find a crowd of people waiting outside. Countless women had joined her in the corridor. The brides of servants and soldiers, ministers and farmers, traders and teachers – from royalty and the roadside. Queen Gandhari and her daughters-in-law stood in solidarity. This was a new morning, wherein the women had come to offer me strength. To not feel dwarfed by the deceit of disgraceful men. The strength to resume life with respect, dismissing the attempts of cowards to shake the ground off my feet. The Kaurav wives applied ointments to the bruises on my skin. They lifted the covers of the bowls carrying hand-made oils from the herbs carefully cultivated in the palace orchards. The aroma pushed open the apprehensive gates of an abused mind. The Kaurav wives entered the room to fill the bath with jasmines and sandalwood, before pouring in warm water. Only Gandhari stood at a distance, joining her hands before me, her head lowered with shame, tears streaming down her face.

'I will not come too close to you, Draupadi,' she cried. 'This morning, every single woman near you will end up giving away her secret powers to your voracious absorption. The blessings of the goddess have left my sons. All they are left with now is their mother's love. I cannot lose that last possession.' She wiped her cheeks, her voice deep in agony. Mother Kunti looked away stubbornly, unwilling to melt to miserable apologies. Gandhari was inconsolable. Other than lost pride of her throne and womb, she had lost the only friend she had in the family.

The great indignity that transpired in Maha Bharat brought irreversible curses upon the men folk. They would no longer be trusted easily. Faces would be judged, intentions would be questioned. Who knew which heart was camouflaging a lustful Dushasan's sinful desires, waiting to be triggered by one call of the evil? The assault of justice haunted every human living in the times and for generations thereafter.

There was deafening silence all around us. Deadly stillness was interrupted by the sporadic wails of Gandhari. The winds of transformation had started their journey. Krishna's eternal call meandered through the grave nights and stormy days, rambling across valleys and riversides, deserts and plains.

'Krishnaa … Krishnaa … Krishnaa …'

*

A thousand bells clashed against each other. These were the bells of consciousness, reminding the world to stay awake and aware. Turbulent winds raised havoc, pushing the stars behind the black clouds in an overcast sky. Drops of water trickled down my head. Thunder and lightning broke the sky into a million fragments, augmenting fantasies with a flash of the pale light before returning it to darkness eventually. Today Indra was restless, Krishna was watchful.

Somewhere not too near but not far away either, Mother Kunti was praying. I could hear the mathematics of the universe. How independent variables from unrelated orbits came together to inspire significant revolution in a supposedly controlled society. She seemed to be in conversation with the spiritual world, seeking wisdom and strength. Seeking justice. Her voice choked with enormous grief, readying for an immense sacrifice. I walked outwards where her chants were most audible. In another world Indra was sharpening his vajra, raising the shattering sound of the thunder. It felt sacred, when both the father and the mother were in sync. The soft drizzles soon made way for heavy rains. After a long time since I moved away from Panchal, I was graced once again by the touch of the doting patriarch caressing my open hair.

'Devraj Indra … where are you? … talk to me, please!'

I called out loudly at the trees lashing against each other, the raging winds whistling past me. The dry leaves and floating bits stopped mid-air, shocked at my direct call to Indra – audacious and abrupt. Lightning tore through the sky. Opaque layers shoved apart. The Devraj was seated on a majestic cloud, its colours fading from turquoise to grey, with shiny silver lining its contours. The stormy winds grew pleasant; trees stooped forward to shelter me from the devastating downpour. My words lost, I stared at the celestial stunner, dressed in pristine white like Mother Kunti. Pearls from the oceans hung from his neck. He shimmered as if one touch would melt him into water. The Godfather smiled kindly, placing the vajra on his side. 'I am hearing you, powerful.'

'Me? Powerful?' I repeated, breaking away from the captivating daze. 'I wish I had taken the advice of Mother Kunti seriously and learnt the use of my body and arms. What began in the Hastinapur court would have concluded there.'

'What good would that have done?' Indra refuted. 'Personal wars are many in this world. People fought with their heads and limbs, and they fought until they could fight no longer. No one heard about those sacrifices. Draupadi's battle has got people talking. They will talk more in the days to follow, as the civilized and the wild will witness the biggest war for justice.'

'I would have celebrated the grandeur of Draupadi, if only I was not Draupadi.' I sighed. Why wasn't I just another woman, content in the company of her man, loved by humans and nature alike? Why is happiness always cursed?

Cold streams of monsoon ran down my torrid scalp. The God returned no response. A chariot takes a few hours to travel from Panchal to Kurukshetra. The same distance had cost me half a lifetime.

'The sins inflicted upon innocence can transform the harmless into a monster.' He spoke after a long silence. 'Else, the sufferings leave people questioning their lifelong faith, their original convictions irretrievable. Who other than Draupadi could walk through the brutality and still have her wisdom unfazed?' A tide of moist winds touched my forehead. 'Draupadi has set an example for the future.'

I nodded quietly. These were pleasant words. But I missed the world I had left far behind. The homes I made in the Dvaita forest, in the Hastinapur palace, at Indraprastha. How would it be if I was not the chosen one to represent the battles of the oppressed! Why couldn't I be left alone with my choices instead?

'I wish I was anonymous,' I said. 'I thought my life would be an illustrious fable, in which I would feature as a happy character. The fact that such fables are a myth is shattering.'

In my dreams, Arjun and I were still together, hand in hand, beside a pond covered by lotus leaves. Arjun would tease me saying the lotus scent of my body was stolen from the poor buds. I would jump into the water to return the wealth. Arjun would dive after me. In reality, Arjun was my convict. Our delightful lotus pond had turned into a thorny trench – I had been pushed into it. Arjun mourned. Neither could he avert my fall, nor remain the partner who was committed to share everything. The man was incapable of perceiving this pain of his woman.

'There is one fundamental error in your theory. Fables don't have happy characters, only visionaries and villains. You are indeed an intriguing character from a legendary fable,' Indra insisted. I smiled. Indra was kinder than Krishna. He kept honey-coating the severe truths for me.

'Do you know, your desire for Arjun shook the catalogues of destiny in heaven? My son went places, conquered many, married more than once, but couldn't become a husband ever again.'

This was not something I wanted to talk about. I was not at ease with my husband's marital status. Indra's words led to an awkward silence, until he broke it himself.

'Your longing made his nights sleepless. The winds, my agents, carted to him your messages of love and disappointment. Effortlessly, you energized the palace of Hastinapur, exfoliating the stones and the corners that had forgotten the magic of human touch – existing and operating like automated machines. Bhishma's fondness for you invoked jealousy among those who had done nothing to achieve his affection but felt entitled to it. Terrorized, the Evil conspired to kill your capacity to love. In desperation, Duryodhan and his allies upturned an already overflowing pot of sins, which will now bring doom upon them. If you are not a mythical icon, who is?'

Indra stopped, waiting for me to process the information. The words percolated slowly. True, it was. Who says myth is the magic of the past? Life itself is the biggest myth. Unbelievable sufferings are transformed into incredible ballads after a traumatic phase is left behind.

But not all myths are tragic. Magnificently contrasting was the Pandav faculty, which eloquently illustrated Indra's aesthetic brilliance.

'Myths are such.' The Devraj had followed my chain of thoughts. 'They are the stories of spectacular accomplishments coupled with helpless tears.'

'Tears?' I was surprised. 'What regret would you have, Devraj?'

'Only one regret,' he confessed. A cluster of clouds glided past him, coloured with hues of violet, black, orange and white. A few clung on to Indra's shoulders like possessive devotees singing dedicated hymns. He plucked them gently and assembled them into gigantic chunks prepared for downpour. 'I couldn't father my son the way a father does. The privilege was taken from me and given to Pandu. I stole an opportunity when the Pandav were exiled to the forest after the dice match at Hastinapur. Arjun performed rigorous penance to learn the war strategies of the devas. Briefly, he had visited Amravati at the end of the austere study. In those limited hours, I showered on him everything that shines in the custody of Indra.'

'A father's house, floating in the love preserved for his son. Wasn't he overwhelmed?' I asked, wondering how the union must have been for a celestial father and his terrestrial son.

'He was respectful, though estranged,' the Devraj recollected. 'His destination was Draupadi. Amravati was a temporary stop, piled with boons he didn't want. He kept changing sides on a bed softer than feathers, to rather lie beside Draupadi on coarse grass.'

Why did Indra say *piled with boons*? Did Arjun too have unwanted blessings imposed upon him and he didn't know what to do with them? Blessings that were worse than curses?

I remembered the gory days right after our exit from Hastinapur. The recent past had ploughed many invisible sores on our skin. After the disgrace of the Hastinapur court, Dhritarashtra got frightened. He experienced ominous outbursts from his own people. The days had filled with such a smog that even the blind was affected. He set my husbands free from the bewitched custody of the Kaurav. He gave them back their kingdom but attached the condition of another game of dice. Shakuni was convinced that it was a fair proposition. Yudhishthir lost again. We were exiled for thirteen years under the terms laid by the Kaurav. Twelve years of expulsion and one year of concealment. If we were recognized in the last year, the whole period of exile would have to be repeated. If we fulfilled the conditions successfully, we would get Indraprastha back. We abandoned our royal uniforms and set out for the Kamyak Forest. Arjun went away for an indefinite period, for atonement and penance. He promised to return with finer skills, lethal weapons and divine endowments. I had gratified him with not a single word. He left, looking back for as long as he could. I was turned away from him, working through the chores dispassionately.

'He came back as a transgender, Brihannala!' My voice drowned in a thunderous roar across the amorphous sky.

Sigh of the Devraj sent stormy winds. 'Yes, the unfortunate man returned with Urvashi's curse. The one desired by many refused to pleasure the most beautiful nymph from Amravati.' Godfather Indra mentioned. 'Much later, standing below a large tree outside the kingdom of Matsya, he admitted to have learnt something that he hadn't from all his rigorous research of a lifetime. Brihannala exposed to him the covert pains of Draupadi, which he could never comprehend as a man!'

Some disclosures are ironical towards stupid presumptions. They are both unsettling and blissful. Arjun never told me about this. Brihannala, the ever-smiling eunuch, taught dance to Princess Uttara, daughter of King Virat of Matsya kingdom. We had taken shelter in his palace during our year of hiding.

Mother Kunti didn't accompany us to the forest. Before beginning the long journey when I'd bent down to touch her feet, she held me tightly with her palms on my shoulders. A silent message lay hidden in her eyes. She would be our secret messenger from the palace. Uncle Vidur was always the closest Pandav aide but he couldn't breach the corners reserved for women.

I sent my own children to Dwarka with Subhadra and Abhimanyu. I didn't shed tears on that day. Subhadra did. Gripping my hand within hers, she assured that my children would be her priority. I stared at the beautiful, naughty faces. They stared back, wondering why the relocation was required. I hugged them. Their milky skin would change so much by the time we would meet again. I tried not to think about it. How many children in the country would be so wretched to suffer their mother's fate? Even a beggar was richer than Queen Draupadi.

I knelt down before the sharp and bright Abhimanyu. He put his hands around my neck and repeated after his mother, 'Everyone dear to you will always be my priority.'

My insides shivered with an unknown disquiet. 'When I am back, the best gift I carry with me will be yours,' I told him.

Thirteen years after, I returned with King Virat's daughter Uttara and arranged for her marriage with Abhimanyu, an acclaimed warrior by now with the childlike excitement radiating from a well-built body. As patient as his mother. As talented as his father. As committed as his maternal uncle.

*

'Why had you called me, Draupadi?' Devraj Indra asked, breaking through the trance of recent memories.

What would I have said? That I just wanted to talk, that I needed someone to listen to me? That I was looking for a stranger and not someone from the world I was acquainted to? A presence before which I could bare my vulnerabilities without fearing of shame?

Wouldn't the master illusionist recycle my fragile vulnerabilities into invincible power?

'Advise me, Devraj Indra. How can I be of use in the historic war of Kurukshetra?' I said with a hopeful heart. The aura around him brightened with a series of lightning flashing across the sky. He smiled as if this was all he wanted to hear.

'I will tell you when it is time,' he assured. The enchanting shine on his serene face, however, implied something already was brewing.

15

One lifetime. So many memories. So many people to love. Only one heart.

In all these years, Arjun could never have enough of me, and I, him. At different times of our life, I saw a different side of him. Sometimes, he came to me as the gentle Yudhishthir. Some days, he was the muscular, childlike Bhim, sharing my love for food and feeding others. The handsome Nakul filled my senses with everything beautiful that a woman could long for – even dreams carried the fragrance of his charm. There would also be the long nights when the flickering lamp would cast long shadows behind Sahadev, the knowledgeable one, filling me with the depth of his intellectual expeditions. Arjun appeared like fresh blooms, laced with thorns. As long as he'd be there, he'd envelop his beloved with his love, touching intimately. After hours of fervent passion, he'd suddenly be gone. I tried new ways to keep him engaged for longer. He escaped those entrapments, returning when I expected him the least.

One man, five shadows – the biggest Pandav secret and the enemy's worst ignorance.

Rejoicing for and revolting against the uncertain mystery called life, where everything goes away and comes back in due course, where every Karma meets its muse and every truth finds its voice, I sat in silence, falling back and coming out of the bygone days. The people and their love. The journeys and their merits. My birth and my marriage. My parents and my in-laws. Tremendously eventful. Extraordinarily dull.

I often thought about Mother Kunti's parting advice to me before we went on exile. 'These thirteen years will be the time of great opportunities to study the occult and experiment with the unexpected, to bond with the indigenous and understand the wild.' I believed, this was also the period of great resolve, to serve the earth and the earthlings, to connect back to the self and reinstate the shaken trust, to observe penance and seek blessings. Together, we travelled places, eradicated many a corrupt existence from the face of the earth, liberated the captives and brought joy to the natives. We learnt, discovered and befriended communities that were no less enthralling than the bejewelled city of Indraprastha on the banks of the Yamuna. Mayasur had said, 'Wherever Draupadi goes, the palace of illusion will follow.' His prophecy surprised me pleasantly. The magic of the palace soothed my troubled nerves, bestowed hope amid strange circumstances, screened before my eyes any part of the world as I willed. It kept me in constant touch with my lover. I saw my children growing steadily with Abhimanyu, under Subhadra's profound care. I heard Mother Kunti praying for us.

When Arjun left for his research, I didn't

bother to bid him goodbye. But my life stopped until he came back as Brihannala, having been cursed by Urvashi.

'Why didn't you give her what she wanted?' I asked later.

'I would like to believe that men too have the right to own their bodies and their minds,' he grimaced.

'Tell me more,' I nudged.

He hesitated before speaking up. 'Urvashi's lust for me was as mortifying as Shakuni's for you.'

Without waiting for further questions, he climbed up a tree to hide the celestial Pandav weapons before we entered the kingdom of Matsya to spend our thirteenth year in disguise as the servants of King Virat.

When we returned and claimed Indraprastha back after fulfilling all the conditions imposed by the Kaurav, they resorted to chicanery once again, unwilling to hand over the kingdom. The Pandav declared war to retrieve their respect and dignity. The open grounds of Kurukshetra situated on the north-west of Hastinapur was chosen as the battlefield.

*

The night was transcendental. The Yamuna slapped large boulders of rocks on its way and deposited the dilapidated remains on its sides. The soil on its embankment was known to be fertile. Is every collapse as prolific? The Yamuna didn't fret about what it decomposed and what was rebuilt. The fish bred in its eternal flow; the water provided for livelihood across tribes. Boats waited to be ferried in the morning, their head on land and the tail in the water. Red flowers of the gulmohar bent from above, some of them slipped onto the wooden ports. I picked up a handful. They were fresh and wet. But the end was evident, and the end was near. Blossoms never mourn; they wilt away with grace.

From afar, the kingdom of Indraprastha waved at its erstwhile queen. Standing on my toes, I stretched to take a broader look at the expansion.

Were the people doing well? Was there an abundance of flora and fauna? Were the trade routes suitably maintained? Did people have enough to eat and enjoy? Did the monsoons visit on time? Indraprastha responded to none of my questions. The kingdom looked haunted, its reflection breaking into the ripples of the Yamuna. I found in the muddled mirror all the truth that Maya had left to be revealed on its own.

The Takshak visited every day to destroy a little of Maya's magical architecture. He took the waterway, planted corrupt thoughts in the minds of the people. It spat in the water when they dipped their drinking pots in the Yamuna. Jealousy, anger and suspicion was being administered to sedate intelligence, unsettle pursuits, disable focus and impair loving, creating and sharing. When the people would be sufficiently isolated, he'd approach in disguise, pretending to be one of them. No one would recognize the forgotten Khandav chief. His intervention would be slow, but he'd persist. Seldom is anyone more patient than the evil.

Every illusion is subject to distortion, and eventually destruction. So will this palace and the *Maya Nagari*. Centuries after, it would feature as a legend in folk tales recited by aging raconteurs while putting naughty children to sleep. Maya always said, 'Art is an illusion. Indraprastha is art.' The day Takshak succeeded in influencing the subjects, Indraprastha would lose its balance. The foundation would be destabilized below the river. Ages and ages hence, when generations would have passed, Takshak would still seek his revenge and witness with malevolent pleasure the drowning of the illustrious Indraprastha into the mighty Yamuna, never to be discovered again by any advent of archaeology.

Pulled out of my eerie reverie, I turned towards Hastinapur on the other side. There was too much noise there, too many voices, waiting for the ultimate silence.

'My fidelity with the royalty will never be compromised. But the vitality of Devavrat is treasured in the caskets of Draupadi. I will still fight till the last breath. Heartfelt blessings for all my grandchildren.'

An informer visited this morning with news of Bhishma's closed-door meeting with Dhritarashtra, where he had laid before the king a balance sheet of the resources for war. 'Before appointing me as the army general of the Kaurav, you must know that Bhishma is physically awake but spiritually dead,' he warned.

Dhritarashtra, in return, had expressed his displeasure for the way the narratives were spiralling beyond his control. He advised that these events had been willed by God and mankind should bow before them. Bhishma had smiled. 'I'm afraid, King of Hastinapur, you are incapable of hearing God's will. Your son's will sounds like God's to you. I'd pray for the repercussions to be milder than you deserve.'

The meeting ended there.

My eyes brimmed with tears. Would I get to see Bhishma again? Would he remain the kind and loving granduncle-in-law? Would I get to feed him again with my culinary offerings that he loved so much? I prayed for his well-being, for his long life. How much resentment could I hold for the elderly man, who contributed to the humiliation of the throne with his silence but was too feeble to see through it? Did he realize that his venerable vow of protecting the throne had been assaulted? I prayed for the repercussions of this too to be milder than he deserved.

The next day, we travelled to the Upaplavya city in Matsya, where the Pandav had camped with their allies. My father was among the first to join, along with Dhrishtadyumn and Shikhandini. Dressed for war, she had chopped off her hair and donned an armour covering her body and back. She called herself Shikhandi. Other armies and their leaders allying with us travelled from Kasi, Matsya, Kekaya, Magadh, Chedi, Pandya and many other small places. Individuals and groups befriended by the Pandav at various phases of exiles arrived with daggers, spears and arrows dipped in wild poison, from glaciatic wetlands, barren deserts, remote forests and even underwater. Life was abuzz with its irony.

*

In seclusion, I lay looking up at the ceiling. The thick cloth ceiling turned transparent to screen the black, overcast sky devoid of stars. The morning hours had arrived but the world was still enveloped in darkness. The breeze was sparse, the owls awake, the leaves of the trespassing branches motionless. Sleeping birds inside the quiet cavities of trees were woken up by obnoxious harbingers signalling the arrival of dawn. Porcupines stealthily climbed up the uneven trunk of a peepul tree, only to race back down upon spotting a deadly viper coiled up on the topmost branch, waiting lazily for a prey to walk into its snare. The bats were having a noisy reunion.

At our camp, the Pandav supporters observed tranquil silence before the storm, rejuvenating themselves with prayers, filling their quiver with the choicest of weapons.

My blazing body, calm on the outside but shivering with tremendous passion, felt the touch of Arjun. We only had this much time to ourselves, before he began his journey to Kurukshetra. Holding me dearly in his arms, Arjun submitted once again, apologizing for the inactivity of the Pandav at the royal court. He knelt with despair, seeking forgiveness, pleading me not to renounce my love.

I forgave him finally for the impotence of one morning.

With the first rays of the sun touching the earth, I smeared his forehead with rakta chandan. He rode his chariot and galloped away. His army followed. Dust storms left behind by the daunting warriors turned the air opaque. I returned to my tent.

The war of Kurukshetra would set a lasting tradition for everything that qualify as virtues and vices in the country. We were not at liberty to make mistakes. I prayed, seeking collaboration with the deity under whose abundance the Devlok blossomed.

Thin rays of light penetrated the dark tent. Cold, moist hands bestowed blessings.

'Draupadi, the time has come to reorganize your partnership with Arjun. Kurukshetra is calling. Listen to the invitation of the mystic.'

I lowered my head, bowing before Indra. The hours were inching towards the shakra amavasya, when the moon lay in Indra's star, vishakha.

'Invoke within you the strength that the women had left with you that night.' Devraj Indra whispered into my ear, reminding me of those fateful hours when I had locked myself inside a chamber of Hastinapur. 'You are the custodian of the most lethal weapon that no deva can match, no human can counter. Assemble them before the war begins. Solicit the power of the feminine wrath. You are to grace Arjun's quiver.' The tent went back to its darkness.

I closed my eyes and called upon the energies bestowed by the solidarity of the women. Remorseful eyes of the Kaurav wives had disclosed lost love, disowning their husbands who had fallen from the position of pride. Their dejection and their compassion, preserved somewhere inside me, woke up with a jerk, filling my insides with such fire that the fire-born hadn't experienced before. The overflowing vigour radiated from my body, my complexion shining black, palms blood red. A mysterious woman rose from her slumber, Panchali was pushed behind. Naked she stood, forsaking the cover of every emotion that bars a mission from taking its flight.

EPILOGUE

'Shouldn't we leave, Godfather?' I asked impatiently.

'Not yet.'

'Why!' The army had reached the battlefield already. I was still grounded afar.

'Arjun is in grave sadness, Draupadi. He is stranded alone, caught in the first phase of the battle. If he emerges victorious from the internal dilemma, he will be invincible at Kurukshetra. If he falls today, he will die many deaths. No win will ever match up to that loss.'

Shuddering, I threw my hands out trying to touch Indra. The magnificent illusion kept himself away from my reach. 'Why is he sad,

Devraj? Which internal battle are you talking about?'

'The battlefield that Arjun must ravage soon is full of his loved ones,' Indra explained. 'Some that taught him to love and laugh, some who hand-held him to climb steep stairs, those who filled his childhood with stories of peacocks and the rakshas, the ones who taught him to lift the bow and aim an arrow, those that contributed to his confidence and inspired him with their life force. They are all out there, standing in opposition. He feels demoralized and hopeless.'

I clutched onto the door of the tent. Arjun's dilemma was deep and destructive. This vacuum was not for me to fill. He would have to face it alone. Mother Kunti was right. No level of intimacy could split one's personal battles. Krishna remains the only companion, everyone else drifts apart.

'Arjun is in the midst of the most divine exchange. His impulse is having a conversation with his conscience.' The words of Devraj Indra were ambivalent. Yet they were profound.

Resigned into a few moments of silence, I tried to gather the full meaning. Indra was the impulse of humans. Arjun was the son of the great Indra. Krishna, his trusted friend, was the conscience.

Was Arjun conferencing with Krishna?

'Yes, Arjun is with Krishna,' the Godfather revealed. 'His impulse, borne by Indra, tells him to withdraw. Krishna, his conscience, reminds that these loved ones had forsaken him at the most crucial hour of his life, sticking to their own vows, vices and Dharma.'

'Who will win the negotiation, Devraj?' I asked solemnly.

'Indra is often overruled by Krishna. It won't be any different today.' The declaration came without hesitation.

In the world outside, the trees moaned, frogs croaked, crickets chirped and owls hooted. Was the nature in pain as were humans? Or was it an undertaking of recovery? How did life move on even when the mind was strangled?

'After every storm comes the revitalized sunlight.' Indra refused to encourage my cynicism. 'Arjun is preparing for a dauntless ride. His impulse will engage in the battle from the chariot. The conscience will be his charioteer. The most divine collaboration will translate between Parth and Parthsarathy. *Nara* and *Narayana*. Man and *Bhagwan*.'

Thunder broke through the sky, accompanied by the majestic lightning. The mortal world was startled with the celebratory euphoria in the cosmos. The jubilance of Indra unfurled like the flow of a mighty river.

'This dialogue between the impulse and the conscience will be treasured as the timeless reference for the earthly and the unearthly. It will resolve difficult dilemmas on personal and social truth, retracking every lost path back to righteousness. It will be called the Gita.'

*

The sky was cleaning up. The clouds were breaking off like bereft cotton from a thick blanket and refilling the void with darker silhouettes. I heard the loud call of Krishna's conch. Melodiously, it blew. Once, twice and thrice. Arjun was done.

Indra stretched his hand. Colours from different corners dashed into his grasp. He threw them up in the air. They arranged themselves in lines curving as the magnificent rainbow on the sky, touching the horizon before us and elongating itself high up in the air. With a charismatic smile pasted on his face, he invited me to ascend the *Indra-dhanush*. On the other end of the regal hepta-colour arch, the battleground of Kurukshetra was seething in intense thrill.

This was the phase of annihilation for the Evil, for the Dharma of humanity to restore its order. Wherever I stepped on the dry grounds, the soil charred and black smoke of the crematorium raised its plumes. The burning smell of human flesh filled the air. Behind me walked many others, the spirit of the oppressed from real and occult worlds, their footsteps gallant like the swift horses of war. The silent warriors pledged loyalty to the Pandav confederation. They followed in solidarity towards the artifice that attempted to victimize the harassed, sparing the culprits.

I saw Bhishma lying amid the burns, both

his hands holding large swords dipped in blood, his body pricked by a thousand arrows carrying Arjun's symbol inscribed in the tail. The victorious laughter of Shikhandi echoed in the air.

Further along the path, I heard the last wails of Dronacharya before he was slayed by brother Drishtadyumn.

Where was my father hiding away from the mortal world now?

Not very far away, a glorious warrior rode forward, his horse steady, face tranquil and radiance inspiring. He looked bare. Karn stopped a few yards ahead of me.

'Both I and Arjun wanted you, Draupadi,' he said, breaking the ice walls between us. 'I had seen you travelling in a palanquin in Panchal. You had climbed out of it when it rained. Shikhandini's question in an open auditorium felt shameful. My rival played it up as a rare honour. I was stationed outside the auditorium till the end, hoping to be called in when all kings failed.' He continued sadly, 'Someday, I thought, Draupadi would want me. When that never happened, jealousy stung me like a scorpion. An unknown monster raised its head and I failed myself.' He held his face down in remorse.

'Where are your kavach-kundal?' I called out. Without the ornaments that always adorned his chest and ears, he looked different.

'Those were the protective covers gifted by my father.' Karn lifted a hand to touch his chest. 'I have shed every armour that Arjun doesn't have. I will fight him for the first and the last time today as an equal.'

His face shone with ultimate fulfilment. He was approaching the moment he had waited for all his life.

'Before you stands a dauntless warrior, a silent lover and a disoriented antagonist.' He lowered his head again. 'If you can, don't remember me by my last identity. No apology can express the dishonour I brought upon myself. In your ability to forgive, may my incompetence dissolve.'

He resumed his ride towards the battlefield.

Shrieks of Mother Kunti reverberated all across the place, calling out for someone to stop him. No one did. By the recline of the Surya a few evenings later, Karn faded away.

Standing inside his armoury, Arjun said that the Agni hadn't just gifted him the Gandiv but also the arrow that was to couple with it. I didn't understand then that he meant me. I walked straight through the ruins as people and horses fell on both sides amid mourning screams. I didn't turn. The Gandiv had twanged. The catastrophic weapon was speeding forward, leaving behind destruction and carnage. An arrow never looks behind; humans do.

The laments of Arjun tore through the haze of devastation. Vultures flew further away, poisonous snakes retreated inside their holes, lions dashed away like the deer. The wild mourned the savagery of civilizations. For all these years, unlike all I have seen and known, the tears of Krishna splashed over my skin. My eyes were moist too, grief flowing uninterrupted with the death of the bravest warrior from the Pandav camp. The youngest of them all. My body shook. The earth trembled.

*

Who am I?

The question that troubled me so much once didn't matter anymore.

My identity had transformed too many times, from a daughter to a wife to a mother; the queen of Indraprastha and a servant at Matsya; a weapon, finally. The arrow with a mind of its own. I have been told that all of these aside, I had another dominating identity. I am a *Sati*. The one who is pure and resolute, fearless and liberated, loyal yet sovereign. I heard Mother-in-law Kunti was a *Sati*. So was Mandodari, the queen of Lanka and the daughter of Mayasur, the magical architect of our lofty Indraprastha.

Who creates such titles and such categories, I wonder. I wanted to ask the creator, what was the need to recognize a handful of women as the more powerful ones, in comparison with those who may have unfortunately succumbed to their circumstances? Did the master of such titles know enough about the arduous life-journeys of women? The tenderness that must walk through the garden of sharp nails planted by friends and enemies alike? The minds that function with warm indulgence and stern authority, forgiving often but forgetting never?

Would history recall Draupadi as the enthusiastic homemaker committed to rehabilitate the dark corners of her beloved country? Would the colossal erosion of a cheerful queen be acknowledged? Or would she be retconned as the epitome of devastation, causing the death and destruction of worthy warriors in an epic? Would anyone ever know that all Draupadi wanted from her life was a home and happiness – trusting, providing and nourishing everyone who crossed her path?

Only time would tell. Or perhaps it wouldn't.

ACKNOWLEDGEMENTS

I must begin with the readers. Thank you for the generous response to the Sati series. For connecting with me across various social media platforms and expressing your delight. For raising questions and for recommending the works to more readers and forums. I am overwhelmed.

I must especially mention here the Instagram artists whose creativity mesmerizes me. The way you photograph the book/s on the window-sides and the tables, adjust the light and shade in ravishing proportions, add the pearls or plants, spread zari or laces – they make for a terrific afterstory, which leaves an author humbled and grateful. You guys are fabulous. I am thankful for your reviews.

I am thankful to the very predictable life with magic at unknown turns, when sudden occasions and conversations (or the lack of it) reinforce ancient philosophies. They are recycled as resources in my writing.

In the course of my journey with Draupadi, I am immensely thankful to the team of Pan Macmillan India – Teesta, Isha, Rajdeep, Bharti, Ditsha and Vijay. I can't stop missing Dr Prasun Chatterjee, with whom the journey had begun.

Big thanks to Misha for coming up with the wonderful jackets for the books.

My sincere gratitude to author–economist Bibek Debroy for his tremendous support and encouragement. He is the knowledge bank that settles many of my confusions gracefully.

Author friends – Saikat Majumdar, Kiran Manral, Saiswaroopa Iyer, Damyanti Biswas, Anuja Chandramouli and Utkarsh Patel – much thanks for your constant support and for producing excellent work from your own tables, which inspire me immensely. Saikat, thank you for the beta-reading and the long conversations which make me think more critically. Senior authors – Namita Gokhale and Chitra Banerjee Divakaruni – I am a distantly placed learner with a voracious appetite for your books. Your writing is my homework.

Thanks to my mother, Ratna Dasgupta, for agreeing and disagreeing with me on diverse topics. Things that I want to tell her, but don't, sometimes slide in as dialogues in the stories.

My husband, Tuhin A. Sinha, never reads my manuscripts till they come back in a book form (and vice versa). But during the writing stage, we share ideas and hold debates, questioning each other's thoughts, ideas and ideologies. When Google fails to provide an apt synonym, he is my go-to person.

My son, Neev Tanish – I owe to him my writing career.

ALSO IN THE SATI SERIES